Fiona

ALEX WAGNER

THE CURSE OF THE CAT GODDESS

A Case for the Master Sleuths

1

It was I who found the dead man.

He was lying at the foot of the big staircase in the hall, and I sniffed out who he was immediately, even before I could go around and look at his face: Tobias Unruh, the owner of the villa where we had been guests for the last three days.

We—that is, my cat Pearl and my two humans, Victoria Adler and Tim Mortensen, and of course yours truly: Athos, proud descendant of the wolves of Alaska, and the leader of our little pack. (Pearl would claim the opposite of course, but *you* are not fooled by that, right?)

The house was as silent as a tomb and, apart from a dim light burning in the hall, pitch black. The night was already quite far advanced; in a few hours the morning would dawn, but Tobias would not be alive to see it. Never again.

I howled in fright and to raise the alarm, to wake the other two-leggeds in the house from their sleep. Then I collected myself and cautiously approached the corpse.

I smelled blood, but it was only coming from the dead man's nose. I listened for his breath, for a heartbeat, but there was nothing—nothing but silence.

When he was alive Tobias had been a sturdy man in

his late forties, with the dark, bristly hair of the rough-haired dachshund type, and friendly blue eyes. Now his gaze was fixed and blank, and he looked as if his own death had surprised him.

Apart from the bloody nose, I could detect no open wounds on his body. I lowered my muzzle until it touched his face, but I had not been mistaken; Tobias Unruh was dead as a doornail.

What a strange saying of the two-leggeds: *dead as a doornail*. How could such a thing ever have been alive in the first place, and therefore able to die?

Anyway, there was no time for any further philosophical reflections of this kind, for suddenly a two-legged who was very much alive appeared behind me and started shouting hysterically at me. "Away with you, you horrid cur! What the hell have you done?"

The two-legged's name was Ivo Lindquist, and he had been a close friend of the dead man. He did not dare to actually approach me and push me aside, but instead he waved his arms wildly and continued to berate me, trying to drive me away.

I don't even want to repeat here the swear words and invective he threw at me. He was very rude indeed. I had to stifle a warning growl.

Since I am quite a good-natured dog, I did him the favor of retreating from the corpse. He immediately rushed toward the dead man, went down on his knees next to him and clumsily started groping his neck, probably looking for a pulse.

Then he yelled for help. "Come quickly! Tobias—Tobias is dead! This dog attacked him."

He looked over at me and contorted his face into a horrible grimace. Whether it was out of grief over his dead friend, or because he actually thought I was a bloodthirsty monster, I could not say.

Anyway, I couldn't believe my ears. *I* was supposed to have killed Tobias? Was the man out of his mind—not only uncouth, but completely insane?

Well, it wasn't the first time that a two-legged had considered me a threat; I am just that big and strong, and I look like a wolf. And of course I *can* be dangerous, deadly even, when it comes to defending my cat or my humans. I'm certainly not a lapdog, but I don't usually attack people ... not without good reason, anyway. Unless they are murderers, but that's another story.

I'd been sleeping peacefully in the villa's kitchen before I found the dead man, having come down from the first floor some time before.

Victoria and Tim's guest room was up there, and I had begun my night's rest at the foot of their bed, as I was wont to do. Pearl had once again been abusing one of my front paws as her pillow—as *she* liked to do—and neither a sound nor the light of the moon streaming through the large windows of the old villa had disturbed our night's rest.

But at some point I had woken up because I felt thirsty. I'd pulled my paw carefully out from under

Pearl's head, for which I'd gotten an ill-tempered hiss—but Pearl had complained without waking up. She'd simply slept on while I quietly slipped out of the room. Victoria was snoring away in the bed, while Tim's breaths were barely audible even to my dog's ears.

I'd run down the stairs in the villa's great hall, turned into one of the corridors and directed my steps into the kitchen. There was my water bowl—well, more precisely, *our* water bowl, because Pearl was allowed to use it too, of course—although for her it was rather more the size of a swimming pool. Pearl is a half-portion of cat, even though she has the ego of a royal tigress.

So I'd sipped some water and then spontaneously decided to make myself comfortable for a bit on the wonderfully cool tiles of the kitchen floor. Upstairs in the bedroom the floor was covered with fitted carpet, and the late summer nights were still very warm. Here in the kitchen, the thick walls of the old house and the tiled floor provided a pleasant coolness, perfect conditions for a dog whose coat is designed for Arctic temperatures.

In short, the little nap I'd wanted to take downstairs had turned into a longer snooze—until at some point a noise had jolted me out of my dreams. A clinking, as if some glass object were breaking into a thousand pieces.

It took me a moment to shake off my drowsiness

and realize where the sound had come from: the dining room, I decided, which was directly adjacent to the kitchen. I am a sled dog, not a guard dog, and this was not the house of my own two-leggeds, for whose safety I am responsible, but nevertheless Tim and Victoria were sleeping here under this roof. And Pearl, too, who likes to act like an invincible predator, but in truth is just as dependent on my protection.

So I ran to the door, which had closed behind me earlier. I stood on my hind legs and was able to push down on the handle with my muzzle, thus getting out into the corridor. I took a left turn there and repeated the procedure with the dining room door.

I had hardly entered the room before I realized what had caused the clinking that had woken me up.

The glass pane of one of the large patio doors was broken. There were plenty of shards on the floor just below it, and I kept a proper distance so as not to step on one of them. A second door, at the other end of the very spacious dining room, led into the entrance hall. This door was only ajar, not closed.

Had a burglar entered the villa?

It's possible, I said to myself, because Tobias Unruh had something like a private museum, and it was located here in the house. It was a collection of Egyptian art and antiquities, which was very valuable in the eyes of the two-leggeds. Humans, after all, appreciate ancient things very much, as is well known. It is only well-matured bones that they know nothing about, because their teeth are so terribly atrophied.

Of course, I'd immediately taken it upon myself to apprehend the villain who must have entered the house, to prevent him from taking anything.

So I'd hurried from the dining room and into the hall—where I'd come across the body of Tobias at the foot of the stairs. But there was no trace of a burglar. I'd howled out of shock at my discovery of the corpse—and of course also to alert the occupants of the house.

Unfortunately, I hadn't heard anything of Tobias's fall. The kitchen was located quite a distance away from the entrance hall, the door had slammed shut behind me after I'd entered, and the walls of the old house were, as I've said, very solid.

If I hadn't fallen asleep on the pleasantly cool floor, I would have registered something of the fall, like the man's impact at the foot of the stairs, in spite of everything. I was sure of that—after all I have good ears. Tobias had probably not uttered a scream, otherwise I would certainly not have missed it.

Yes, and then ... Ivo Lindquist had showed up, turned quite hysterical and actually accused *me* of murdering his friend. I have already reported about that.

His cries for help finally brought the other inhabitants of the house out of their sleep. Of course I would have been able to do that better than he was able to; after all, my wolf howl is said to be able to wake the dead, but Ivo hadn't given me a chance to apply myself as an alarm siren, apart from my first scream of terror.

So I sat down at some distance from the body, panting because I had become quite hot from the excitement, and pouted. I was supposed to be the murderer? What an insult!

Fortunately, a few moments later Tim appeared at the top of the landing. My human—that is, strictly speaking he was my human's lover, since I belonged to Victoria. Or she to me, whichever way you might like to see it.

Anyway, Tim came rushing down the stairs and let out a startled gasp when he saw the dead master of the house. This sound, however, was nowhere near as hysterical as Ivo's cries for help, or his tirade against me.

"Your dog attacked Tobias!" Ivo promptly repeated his slander against me, this time directed at Tim.

But Tim kept a cool head. He went down on his knees next to the dead man, looked him over thoroughly, without disgust in his gaze, and without giving off the typical odor of human panic. Then he rose and turned to Ivo.

"Nonsense," he said, not unkindly, but still in a firm voice. "You see, Tobias has no injuries whatsoever, except for his nose, which he must have hurt during his fall. Athos didn't attack him; he would never do such a thing."

He looked over at me, and I panted in agreement.

"Quite right," I said, but of course Tim didn't understand me.

I have—just like Pearl does—the persistent habit of talking to our two-leggeds, even though I know very well that our conversations are doomed to be one-sided. Humans do the same with us, and think that we animals are not able to understand their language. Human-animal interaction is characterized by countless terrible misunderstandings.

But let's return to our dead man.

"He must have fallen down the stairs," Tim said, turning to Ivo again. "Just look at his twisted limbs."

Ivo nodded slowly, even though he still gave off a stench of fear and disgust. At least he seemed to have realized that Tim was right, and I was thus vindicated.

2

By the way, it was also Tim to whom we owed our invitation to Tobias Unruh's villa. Tim had originally been a gardener and had spent this summer in Vienna to take part in an entrepreneurship course. Afterwards, he had intended to start his own horticultural business back at home next to our lake.

But things had turned out—as so often in life—quite differently. My former human, the late Professor Adler, had been a historian by training, and had infected the young gardener with his passion for human history. It was why Tim had also visited the city's famous museums during his stay in Vienna. And while there he had met Tobias, who had infected him with his enthusiasm for the culture of the ancient Egyptians after only a very short time. The two men had quickly become friends because of this shared interest.

Their encounter had first led Tim to want to become a historian rather than an independent gardener, and second to cause Tobias Unruh to invite his new friend to stay at his villa, where he housed an impressive collection of Egyptian objets d'art. Victoria, Pearl and I had been allowed to join Tim on this short trip.

Tobias himself owned a cat named Bastet, whom he

had described to Tim as *hospitable*. The joke of the year! But I'll get to that.

Tobias's prized collection contained some very creepy things, for example dried-out corpses that looked as if they'd been wrapped in toilet paper, and which were called *mummies*. It wasn't only humans that had been preserved in this way in ancient Egypt, but also birds, cats, and even the occasional dog. Tobias called several such artifacts his own. In addition, besides a few harmless-looking human-shaped sculptures, he also owned some eerie black statues with jackals' heads that made the fur on the back of my neck stand on end. Not that I was afraid of live jackals—of course not!

Be that as it may. Tim wanted to reorient himself professionally, as the humans called it, and Victoria was also still undecided about her professional future. She had worked as a psychotherapist for many years, treating the wounded souls of other humans, but now this line of work no longer appealed to her.

Just last night I'd heard her say to Tim: "What would you think about me going back to college, too, and getting some training in criminal psychology? After all, we've been getting involved in murders all the time lately...."

In view of the dead man who was now lying at the foot of the stairs, this remark seemed almost clairvoyant.

I spontaneously wondered whether Tobias had really only had an accident on the stairs—the staircase was actually not particularly steep or slippery.

On the other hand humans are known to be incapable of getting back on their paws unharmed after a fall. Pardon, onto their legs, I wanted to say. Even when Pearl, clumsy as she sometimes tends to be, falls from a tree, she always lands on all fours, and at most a few hairs of her fluffy white fur are ruffled. Humans, on the other hand, can sometimes break their necks on a staircase that's not even particularly steep.

Behind Tim, Leo Unruh appeared on the stairs—Tobias's father. When he found his son was dead, he dropped onto the bottom step as if the weight of the whole world were pressing down on his shoulders, and began to cry like a little boy.

"Bastet's curse," he sobbed, burying his face in his hands. "I did warn him, didn't I? More than once! But he wouldn't listen to me..."

Bastet in this case did not refer to the Unruhs' house cat, but let's focus on her for a moment anyway, since she also qualified as a curse in my eyes. She was an Egyptian Mau, a breed that supposedly originated all the way back in the ancient culture on the Nile. Her fur was spotted gray, her eyes green; she was damn fast and agile on her paws, and beyond that, utterly gorgeous to look at. You had to grant her that—but I had never met a more arrogant animal in my entire life.

In ancient Egypt, cats were worshipped as gods— Bastet never tired of mentioning this to anyone who would listen. And to everyone else, too.

Dogs were not even worth a twitch of her whiskers, and even Pearl had only been looked down on with contempt from the beginning of our acquaintance.

Envy, I suspected. Pearl was much smaller, not nearly as nimble and sometimes a bit clumsy. But when it came to beauty and charm, she stole the show from just about every other cat.

At least in my eyes, but then maybe I'm not completely impartial—although most two-leggeds would probably agree. There is hardly a person alive whose heart Pearl can't conquer within a few moments.

"Sooo cute," the two-leggeds like to gush when they see Pearl for the first time. Or, "Oh God, she's unbelievably sweet!" These poor folks are completely unaware of the kind of full-grown domestic tyrant that is really hiding behind the midget's innocent looks.

Anyway, Bastet had greeted us like two intruders in *her* villa when we'd arrived three days ago, and had ignored us ever since.

If we did run into each other, she stared at us with contempt and sometimes even wrinkled her nose, as if I were emitting a particularly unpleasant smell. It had cost me great self-control to not yet have secretly devoured her as a midnight snack. As I've said, I am an extremely good-natured dog.

The constant talk about cat goddesses in this

house—and not only from Bastet's mouth—had gone to Pearl's head. Her ego had grown from the size of a tiger to that of an elephant. So now she was a goddess—and a *catfluencer* to boot. Leo Unruh was to blame for that fact.

The old man now approached his dead son, whimpering and crawling on all fours, to embrace Tobias and shed more tears. None of the two-leggeds stopped him from venting his pain in this way.

However, it crossed my mind that he might be contaminating a crime scene in the process—a grave misdeed in the eyes of any criminal investigator.

The poor two-leggeds, who aren't blessed with such sharp senses as we dogs have, must rely on fleeting traces in murder investigations, on fingerprints and similar things that can easily be destroyed when you hug a corpse—as Leo had just done.

On the other hand, I could not only clearly smell the old man's terrible grief, but also understand it well. What a painful thing it must be to have to bury one's own son!

Regarding the *catfluencer* jibe, let me elaborate: Leo Unruh was a so-called senior citizen influencer who inspired older people on the Internet. He was already over seventy years old, but still a chirpy man, and hungry for the good life. A *best-ager*, as he put it.

And he seemed to be in top shape, too. He worked out daily with his personal fitness coach, and spent the rest of his time filming and photographing himself to entertain his fans.

When Pearl and I had first come into the house, Leo had immediately grabbed onto the tiny one.

"God, she's so cute," he had announced as expected (as almost all two-leggeds do), picking up the kitten and holding her in his arms as he'd started to record his latest video.

Since then at least a half-dozen other film shoots had followed, during which Pearl had been encouraged to assist the old man.

"Cats are all the rage on the internet," she'd announced to me with a puffed-up chest after these sessions. "We increase reach, and win likes and lots of followers!"

What exactly that was supposed to mean she wasn't able to explain to me, but in any case she was now not only a goddess, but also a catfluencer and thus downright obnoxious.

Sometimes I really don't have it easy.

But to finally come back to the *curse of Bastet* that Leo Unruh had been raving about in connection with Tobias's death—it was not about the arrogant house cat, but about a real goddess. To be precise: a millennia-old bronze statue of the Egyptian goddess Bastet that Tobias had added to his collection just a few weeks ago.

The two-leggeds were going bonkers over the statue, and we had no idea why.

In my eyes it was simply a bronze cat, nothing more

and nothing less. It was a little smaller than Bastet the house cat, but its facial expression was at least as snooty.

I am an immortal goddess, her cold gaze seemed to say. *Throw yourselves at my feet, you wretched wimps!*

For Tobias, this statue had been an incomparable treasure and his most prized possession, as he had constantly proclaimed to us, and his guests had also duly and eloquently admired it in his presence.

Humans, what can I say. Not even a psychologist like Victoria can truly explain their often very strange behavior.

Among the people of ancient Egypt, the cat goddess Bastet was considered a symbol of love and fertility, as Tim—quite the budding historian—had informed us.

Cats as symbols of love? Which lunatic thought that up? Surely he had never met a real representative of the species. Here we had yet another example of human weirdness.

In any case, Leo Unruh was of the opinion that there was a curse on the Bastet statue and that Tobias had fallen victim to it. What exactly he meant by this, however, we were to learn only later.

While Leo was mourning his dead son, more and more of the house's residents and guests appeared in the hall. They came hurrying down the stairs from the first floor, dressed in their pajamas or robes, or rushing from one of the corridors on the ground floor. Ivo's screams had apparently gotten them all out of bed.

Every one of them was either frightened when they saw the dead man, or burst into tears—or at any rate seemed shocked by the master of the house's tragic end. No one gave me the impression that they were secretly rejoicing over the passing of Tobias Unruh.

Which was not proof that the man hadn't been murdered.

3

At that moment Ivo Lindquist returned—the slander-er who had accused me of murder. He had disap-peared from my sight a minute or two ago, probably to look around the hall for any clue as to how Tobi-as's tragic death had occurred.

"A patio door has been smashed in the dining room!" he announced excitedly. "Someone must have broken in!" He looked around with jerky head move-ments, his expression distorted by fear, as if he ex-pected that at any moment an armed villain might emerge from a dark corner, or from behind one of the Egyptian statues, sculptures, and columns that were also omnipresent in the entrance hall.

Ivo was from Munich, but seemed to be a frequent guest at the Unruhs' villa. He was a tall, scrawny two-legged, around forty years old, and as enthusiastic a collector as Tobias had been in life. In addition, he had studied history to the doctorate level, which made him a sought-after conversation partner for Tim, who had recently become very interested in the same field of study.

In the past few days Tim had been drilling the poor man with questions, and Ivo had always answered kindly and patiently. Actually, I had found him quite sympathetic—until he'd tried to make me a murderer.

"Then someone broke into the house?" asked Victoria, who had joined us in the meantime. She, too, had taken at closer look at the body, but then sat down next to Leo and tried to offer the old man some comfort.

"Isn't there an alarm system here in the house?" she added in amazement.

"Of course," Leo replied, sniffling. "But we don't activate it when the house is full of guests, or someone will always set it off. And sirens blaring half the night ... that gets annoying."

He wiped his tear-soaked face with the back of his hand and threw Victoria a grateful smile.

"I'll be all right," he said to her, brushing off the arm that she had placed sympathetically around his shoulders.

I tried to imagine a burglar entering the villa. First, he would have had to climb the high wrought-iron fence that surrounded the entire estate. The villa's park was huge and full of old trees, rather overgrown hedges and flower beds, small ornamental fountains—and crowded with Egyptian statues of stone or bronze. Wherever you walked you came across pharaohs with strange headdresses, gods which generally had animal heads, and similar kinds of things.

I was grateful that I hadn't lived in ancient Egypt. A civilization that worshiped cats and jackals as deities, but didn't idolize dogs, and on top of that was ruled by people who also claimed to be gods? No thanks; that was truly not for me.

To come back to the possible burglar: even for a two-legged, who would definitely be superior to us canines when it came to climbing, the fence of the property would be a difficult obstacle to overcome. Especially if on the way back the villain had been hauling away loot. But such a crime was not impossible.

The villa was located in a romantic river valley, which the two-leggeds had christened the *Helenental*. It was overgrown with dense forest, reminiscent of a wild alluvial landscape, and the valley entrance was guarded by the ruins of two castles, allegedly built by robber barons. The nearest small town was called *Baden*, which itself lay about half an hour south of the capital, Vienna.

Tim had raved to us about the millennia-old history of Baden. Apparently it had already been a popular spa in the time of the ancient Romans—and famous for its sulfur springs. The odor was not to be missed.

The Villa Unruh was also quite old. As a dog well-versed in such things, I'd say it was late eighteenth or early nineteenth century, in the typical style of the time, and built of stone and wood, full of gables and turrets. But Tobias—or his ancestors, who had laid the foundations of the Egyptian collection—had gone one step further. They had at least partially *Egyptianized* the house. In other words, there were numerous columns, along with two decorative porches, on the façade, which were supposed to be reminiscent of an Egyptian temple. There was also a large variety of reliefs and murals—inside and outside the building— that were Egyptian in style.

My late professor would have found the mix of styles interesting; he had been fond of such experiments.

In the meantime, Antonia and Seschat Unruh, the last two inhabitants of the villa, had appeared at the foot of the deadly stairs, and Victoria took pains to offer them both comfort as well.

Antonia had been Tobias's wife, and Seschat their daughter. The girl was almost grown up, seventeen years old and almost as much of a pest as Bastet, the house cat. She considered herself extremely cool, spent her father's money hand over fist, and believed that no two-legged over thirty was even half as smart as she was. I don't want to be a nag, but I must note at this point that dog mothers know how to raise their puppies far better than our dear two-leggeds manage to train their offspring.

Now, however, Seschat's casual coolness was gone. She had stormed down the stairs, almost taking a fall herself, and had nestled in Victoria's comforting arms, crying like a little child for her late father.

As for her strange name—as you might have already

guessed—it was also Egyptian. Seschat was the goddess of writing, mathematics, architecture and erudition. In other words, the name suited the girl about as well as Bastet the cat showed a resemblance to a goddess of love.

Seschat wore her light brown hair very short and was a bit chubby; her mother Antonia, on the other hand, had long black hair and probably weighed no more than I do myself. (Which is not to say that I am fat under all this fur; no, Antonia was just very slim for a two-legged, and also a rather small woman). Now she had virtually merged with the wall behind her, pressing her back against it as if she could become invisible that way. She sat there, mute and stiff, on a step a little above her dead husband. She shed no tears and said not a word.

Bastet appeared at the top of the stairs, came strutting down the steps and settled next to Antonia. The latter put a hand on her back and clawed her fingers into her fur.

Bastet remained motionless, stoic, giving comfort to her human by her very presence. I would not have believed her to be so selfless.

For a few moments it was completely silent, then a new cry tore through the feeling of sadness and gloom that had settled over us like a dark shadow.

"Bastet—she's gone! Stolen!"

This time it was Julius Feldmann who came rushing in, also from the dining room. Previously he had stood around motionless and somewhat apart from the other humans, but when Ivo had reported the broken glass pane in the dining room, he had gone to investigate.

Now he rolled his eyes quite dramatically, waved his arms around, and repeated in a shrill voice, "The statue—it's gone. The display case has been broken into!"

I hadn't noticed that at all; the cabinet in question was above my eye level, so I hadn't glanced up at it when I'd walked past the broken patio door earlier.

Julius Feldmann was an art dealer who'd kept selling Tobias special pieces for his collection at regular intervals. At the moment he was a guest at the villa because Tobias had wanted to introduce him to his friend Ivo, who was also a passionate collector, as I've said. Julius certainly hoped to do profitable business with him as well. He was a stocky guy with an almost bald head, more reminiscent of a boxer than an art expert. And apparently he didn't like dogs. Whenever he saw me, he gave me a wide berth. Pffft, such an ignoramus!

Oh, and Julius was the one who had sold Tobias the Bastet statue, by the way, just a few weeks ago. And he apparently believed in a curse emanating from the goddess, as Leo did, although he obviously wasn't that intimidated by it.

Quite the opposite in fact.

Just the day before yesterday, Julius had enthusiastically told Tim and Victoria about the statue's long and troubled history, and the aforementioned curse that he claimed had haunted several previous owners.

Afterwards, Tim had said to Victoria, "I think Julius is just making up these creepy stories because it's good for business. A statue that is cursed ... it would fetch a much higher price than an ordinary one. People just love these scary stories!"

Until the curse strikes *them*.

Leo Unruh, at any rate, took the old tales seriously and was now firmly convinced that Bastet had his son on her conscience.

In case you're wondering how *I* feel about curses in general, and that of Bastet in particular: I could not have said how Tobias had actually died, but I am not at all averse to believing in the existence of curses. Only recently Pearl and I had made the acquaintance of a bad-tempered ghost in another mansion, in another country, owned by another rich family. So why shouldn't the spirits of the ancient pharaohs haunt today's two-leggeds, who were so fond of robbing their graves? Gods are generally even more capricious than spirits, if I'm to believe the statements of my late professor and the documentaries I so enjoy watching on television.

Cats are the most capricious creatures of all, so it's hard to imagine what this cat goddess Bastet might be capable of if you were to incur her wrath.

Victoria abruptly took the floor. "We need to get the police involved," she said, not addressing any particular family member. "Not only for the sake of the stolen statue, but also—well, maybe Tobias's death is related to the burglary. That's fairly obvious, don't you think?"

"You mean the burglar pushed him down the stairs?" asked Tim.

Victoria nodded uncertainly.

"Nonsense," Leo interposed. "There aren't any treasures on the first floor—they're all stored in the rooms down here. What would a burglar want up there?"

"He probably didn't know where anything of value was located in the house," Tim suggested.

Leo fell silent, but looked very skeptical.

Pearl purred next to me. "Excellent," she said, "this is another case for us, Athos. Ever since we arrived here, I've been wondering when the first death would occur. After all, we've been in the house a whole three days already."

"Pearl!" I protested. "How can you say such a thing?"

"What's your problem?" she replied irrepressibly. "It's always been like that up until now, hasn't it? No matter where we go, *boom!* a two-legged drops dead. Or even several of them. Murdered—and then we solve the case catpertly. We're much better detectives than the humans."

"It's called *expertly*," I grumbled. "There's no such word as *catpertly*."

"In my vocabulary, there sure is," she shot back firmly.

"Then you might as well say *dogpertly*."

"Nope, that sounds weird."

I gave up. Any opposition was once again completely futile.

Pearl's most outstanding quality is definitely not her modesty. But as far as these deaths were concerned, which were becoming ever more frequent in our presence, I didn't know how to respond. Unfortunately it seemed she was right about them.

"Maybe it's the gods directing us to the right place at the right time," Pearl mused further. "Bastet and her, um, friends—she leads us to the scenes of crimes that only a cat can solve."

Pearl looked as if she had been served a feast of her absolute favorite food, salmon. The idea that she could be one chosen by the gods seemed to thrill her. But who could be surprised at that.

"A cat, together with a dog," she graciously corrected herself. "You do also play a part in our murder investigations, Fatty. After all, every Sherlock needs his Watson."

My paw whizzed down onto her skull before she could duck away. Gently, of course, but I was most certainly not going to let her get away with calling me *fat*. (Apart from the fact that I didn't want to be degraded to being a Watson.) I had already explained to Pearl at least a thousand times that I only seem a little rounder because I have such magnificent, dense fur. But in vain.

"You brute!" she wailed. "You're always so violent."

"And you're way too sassy than is healthy for you, Tiny," I replied.

"I'm *not* tiny," she protested, lashing out with one of her miniature paws in a flash, sinking her claws into my nose.

"Ouch!" I squeaked like a little puppy.

Now we were even.

4

The next day, Victoria and Tim took a long morning walk with Pearl and me—to clear their heads, as Victoria put it.

We left the villa before breakfast, and walked along the narrow path that meandered through the Helenental. It went over hill and dale, over countless gnarled roots sticking out of the ground, and under a dense canopy of leaves that was already beginning to clothe itself in the colors of autumn.

"I think it'll be just as well if we stay at the Unruhs' house for a few more days," Victoria said. "Like that policewoman asked us to do."

That policewoman was a two-legged perhaps thirty-five years old, with fox-colored hair and narrow dark eyes, who had introduced herself as Chief Inspector Melissa Funke when she'd arrived in the early morning hours.

After Victoria had called the police, two officers in uniform had shown up first. Melissa had appeared later, along with another detective in civilian clothes, whom she'd introduced as her colleague but ordered around like an assistant. His name was Christian Wolf, but he looked more like a young bulldog: slab nose, slightly drooping lower lip, and a head a bit too big compared to his rather lanky body.

However I liked his voice, which sounded friendly and somehow funny, as well as the smell he gave off. He had probably eaten strawberry pie for dinner, or rather for dessert, I noted *dogpertly.* Maybe he had a wife (or a mother?) who was good at baking. Or he liked to be something of a pastry chef himself, when he wasn't playing Melissa's slave and solving murders.

Suddenly a strange thought occurred to me: if Pearl and I were human police officers, would people perceive me as her assistant? Or would it be the other way around, as it should be?

In addition, two more women appeared shortly after Funke and Wolf, to take care of the forensics in the house. However, what with all the activities I wanted to keep track of, and the conversations to eavesdrop on, I didn't have the time to take a closer look at them or their work.

"These two-leggeds are from the Criminal Investigation Department," Pearl explained to me expertly—I beg your pardon, catpertly. "So Tobias's death is suspicious. Certainly he was murdered."

"How would you know, smarty pants?" I asked.

"I've already told you; because we are in the house, and in our presence murders always happen. Which we then have to solve."

What perfect logic!

Melissa Funke asked the humans in the villa some brief questions, which Pearl and I followed attentively. As pets, we had the advantage that no one paid much attention to us, and therefore we could eaves-drop on confidential two-legged conversations with-out any problem at all.

What exactly had happened, Melissa wanted to know. What had the individual residents and guests observed or heard? Where had they been when Tobias Unruh had fallen down the stairs?

The answers were unenlightening and for the most part quite monosyllabic.

In the end, the chief inspector had announced that she and her colleague would return in the morning to have more in-depth discussions. She'd asked all the two-leggeds not to leave the house for the time being, and no one had protested.

We walked, or jogged, respectively, through the beautiful Helenental. The tiny one almost had to gallop to keep up, while I was strolling leisurely be-hind our two-leggeds—which only proved once again that *I* was the leader of our detective duo, as I said to myself with satisfaction.

Chief Inspector Athos, Assistant Pearl. However, I did not dare speak these thoughts aloud. My nose was still smarting from last night.

Tim put his arm around Victoria's shoulders and moved closer to her as he walked. It was not just a gesture of tenderness, but probably also due to the narrowing of the path at this point. It went a little way uphill, past a steep rock face in which there were some small caves.

Since the dense canopy of leaves continued to stretch above our heads, it was quite gloomy and cold. That is, *I* wasn't cold, of course, but Victoria was shivering.

"Why do you want to stay with the Unruhs for a while longer?" Tim asked her. "To provide psychological support to the family? To help them cope with their tragic loss?"

"What?" asked Victoria. She looked lost in thought. "Oh, yes, that too of course." She stopped abruptly and looked Tim straight in the eye.

"I think there's something fishy about this accident Tobias supposedly suffered," she said abruptly. "Doesn't it seem that way to you?"

She didn't give him time to answer, but immediately added, "Ms. Funke thinks so too, I bet. I could see that in her face. Otherwise she wouldn't want to converse with all of us further, would she?"

"And what feels wrong for you about his death?" Tim asked with interest. Victoria's suspicions didn't really seem to surprise him; perhaps he had already been pondering similar thoughts?

"First of all, this burglar, if he really does exist, must have been a real bungler," Victoria said. "He just shatters a window, which would have made a hell of a racket, wouldn't it? Wouldn't a professional have been much more likely to bypass a lock? The locks on

34

the patio doors would be simple for all I know. They don't look like they would be complicated to pick, and that method would be practically silent. Besides, as for Tobias, did he just ... fall down the stairs because he heard the burglar on the ground floor and wanted to check on things?"

"That might be possible, I suppose," Tim said.

"And the burglar then stole just this *one* statue—in a room full of treasures? Was he such a connoisseur that he immediately knew exactly how valuable this Bastet statue is? The thing looked pretty ordinary, if I may say so myself."

"Victoria is doing really well," Pearl told me. "Even though she obviously has no idea about the priceless value of divine cat statues. We've already trained her quite serviceably as a sleuth."

I groaned inwardly.

Of course it was true that Victoria was now quite fond of playing the amateur detective—and so was Tim. But unlike Pearl, I wasn't eager to put our two-leggeds in any danger by goading them into these risky activities.

Tim seemed interested in discussing the case with Victoria. "So if there was no burglary," he said, "and Tobias didn't just slip on the stairs—that would mean he was killed by a family member or one of the houseguests, wouldn't it? In that case, we'd be dealing with a murderer who kept his cool and cold-bloodedly faked a burglary to throw the police off the scent."

"Or perhaps Tobias actually suffered an accident, and someone from the house merely took the opportunity to steal the Bastet statue?" Victoria mused.

The two started moving again, and Pearl and I followed them.

"Who could possibly have a motive to kill Tobias?" Tim continued. "He made a very affable impression on me. I really can't imagine he had any enemies."

He scratched his head, then went on, "Do you think it was about money? That's the number one motive for murder, isn't it? And after all, Tobias was a very rich man. We could discreetly ask who his heirs are—his wife and daughter? Seschat is quite spoiled and simply throws money around, and she really didn't have to murder her father to get her hands on his fortune. Besides, she is still a minor, and presumably her mother will be managing her inheritance at first. And I really don't believe that Antonia will spoil her quite the way Tobias did."

Victoria said nothing in reply, walking on in silence.

Tim gave her a questioning look, but kept up with her and continued his monologue: "As for Antonia ... she's so incredibly quiet. Do you think she's depressed?"

Again, he received no response from Victoria.

He stopped. "Honey? What are you brooding about?"

She walked a few more steps, and only then did

Tim's words seem to get through to her.

She stopped and turned around to face us. Her forehead was deeply wrinkled.

"It's just ... I just remembered an incident," she said. "No, that sounds too dramatic. The matter just struck me as strange, but now—now we may have to look at it in a new light, I'm afraid."

"What matter?" asked Tim.

"Leo—it was two days ago. He was sitting in the garden, browsing the Internet on his cell phone. I happened to walk past him without being noticed, and that's when I saw the kind of page he had accessed. He was in a suicide forum, Tim! And when he heard me, he cringed and closed the page in a flash."

"A suicide forum?" Tim repeated incredulously. "And you think this, um—incident—might have something to do with Tobias's death?"

"I don't know," Victoria said.

She plucked a leaf from a bush growing by the side of the path and crushed it between her fingers, lost in thought. "So Leo is joie de vivre personified, isn't he? In top shape, very engaged in his blogging ... I mean, such behavior can be deceiving, of course, but somehow I can't imagine him contemplating suicide. Or that he'd even want to learn about the best ways to kill yourself and the finer details of each method. After all, that's what such a forum is all about. I memorized the site name and afterwards took a quick look at it myself."

"So you think he might have hatched a murder plot against his own son, and wanted to make it look like suicide?" asked Tim. "Is that what you're getting at?"

"Does that sound crazy?" Victoria asked timidly. "Maybe it was all quite harmless. Although..."

"Crazy—not necessarily. But what kind of suicide was Tobias' death supposed to have been? I mean, who would commit suicide by throwing themselves down a flight of stairs? I've never heard of that. The chances of surviving but possibly ending up in a wheelchair for life are pretty high, I would assume."

"Yes, that's true," Victoria assented. "I don't think you'd fake a suicide like that if you were a potential murderer. An accident, more likely. But not a suicide."

"Agreed," Tim said, "and besides, what possible motive could Leo have for murdering his own son? Surely he won't inherit anything—and if he does, does he really need to? Is he in need of money?"

"I don't know. Is he drawing a large pension? Does he make anything from this influencer thing? I don't even know what he does, exactly."

"I guess he gives lifestyle tips to older men," Tim said thoughtfully. "He does videos on fashion, fitness, nutrition, how to live life to the fullest and make old age the best time of your life. But whether what he does makes any money, I really don't know."

"He certainly seems very strong," Victoria said, "and not merely for his age. He might have pushed Tobias so hard that he broke his neck on the stairs, even though they might not be that steep."

"I don't know," Tim said, "don't we have any other suspects? What about Ivo? Maybe he wanted to steal the Bastet statue, and Tobias found out? After all, Ivo is as fanatical a collector as Tobias was. Perhaps he literally went over a dead body to get this statue into his possession."

"But from the way he's always bragging about his collection and his latest purchases, I got the impression that he's even richer than Tobias," Victoria said. "He could buy any piece he wants, I think, and surely this Bastet statue is not the only one of its kind."

"Hmm," Tim said, "I can't tell—not yet. I'm just starting out, uh, as an historian, I'm afraid." He grinned sheepishly.

But then his face suddenly darkened. "You know what strikes me as strange," he said, then immediately answered the question himself: "Tobias and Ivo, they were close friends, weren't they? At least, that's what they both claimed. And Tobias did treat Ivo like that. But Ivo—I don't know. His friendship seemed a bit forced, I think. Didn't it seem to you that Ivo wasn't really that fond of Tobias?"

"I honestly wasn't paying attention," Victoria said. "I figured Ivo was just a quiet, reserved kind of guy."

I had also gotten that impression of the man myself. But then I remembered that he usually smelled quite stressed. However, I hadn't read too much into that, because the smell is almost standard with humans, it must be said. Their bodies rarely smell of joy and relaxation; quite often they simply reek of stress and anger. Our dear two-leggeds truly have the gift of making life as difficult as possible for themselves.

"Then there's also Julius Feldmann, the art dealer, as a possible suspect," Victoria continued the conversation. "What if he wanted to steal the statue, to sell it a second time? Maybe he had an accomplice who broke into the house specifically to steal that one valuable piece?"

"Well, Julius doesn't exactly strike me as being short of cash either," Tim replied. "The Jaguar he drives easily cost a hundred and fifty thousand euros."

"Maybe he's living beyond his means?" Victoria speculated.

"Or maybe we're just making fools of ourselves here with our Sherlockian games, and it was a real burglar after all, someone who was simply out to get rich? Tobias heard him, tried to confront him, and fell down the stairs in a tragic accident. Maybe we're just being paranoid, sweetie. Don't you think?"

5

Pearl and I listened attentively to our two-leggeds' discussion, but also came up with our own thoughts on the matter.

"Why was Tobias up so late last night anyway?" Pearl asked me, at the same time clambering like a death-defying acrobat over a log that had fallen across the path. I myself had walked over this obstacle without having to lift my paws particularly high.

"Maybe the burglar woke him up?" I suggested.

But that was unlikely. Tobias's bedroom was located on the first floor, almost at the end of a long corridor. It seemed impossible that he could have heard the burglar from such a distance, not even if he'd possessed the hearing of a lynx.

Something struck me at this thought; I came to an abrupt halt.

Pearl, who had just wandered around a puddle of water, turned to me. "What is it?"

"It definitely couldn't have been a burglar who stole the statue last night," I said. "And who may have murdered Tobias."

"*May have*? He was murdered for sure, Fatt— er, Athos. Count on it!" She wrinkled her tiny snout as if to point out to me what a brilliant nose she had for crime. The little show-off.

"Think about it," I said, without acknowledging her little bit of self-aggrandizement, "the timing is impossible. I woke up last night because I heard the glass in the dining room shatter. It took me a very short time to perk up, get on my paws, and tell myself that the sound must have come from there. Then I ran to it; it was just a few steps from the kitchen. I found the broken glass pane—broken from the outside, because the shattered pieces were lying on the floor inside the room. I don't know if the statue was gone by then, because I wasn't paying attention. In any case, I didn't find a burglar. And right after that, I discovered Tobias's body in the hall."

Pearl understood immediately. For a cat, she is actually quite clever.

"That is, if there *had* been a burglar who got in Tobias's way," she mused, as if she were Miss Marple in cat fur, "he would have been long gone by then, instead of just breaking the glass door to gain entry to the house. You're sure you heard the glass break and jumped up right away? You didn't perhaps slumber on a little longer?"

I gave her an indignant look. Such a cheeky remark didn't deserve a response.

At that moment, Victoria called out to us. She and Tim had been walking ahead, but now they'd stopped to check on us. "Come on, you two, don't dawdle!" she admonished Pearl and me.

"Pahh, we're not dawdling," Pearl mewed. "We're

solving a murder here!"

We started moving again, catching up with the humans, but continuing our discussion as we did so.

"There's no way the clinking I heard was caused by a burglar who had just entered the house," I insisted.

"Then this is how it must have happened," Pearl said. "Someone pushed Tobias down the stairs—which is what I've been saying all along—it was murder!—then the perpetrator ran into the dining room, opened the patio door there, and broke the window from the outside. Humans aren't completely stupid, are they? Nowadays, every toddler knows that if you break in from the *outside,* the shards have to be on the *inside.* Then the criminal closed the now-destroyed terrace door from the inside again and disappeared somewhere into the house. Into his room, probably, just before you emerged from the kitchen. In other words, the burglary was staged and the murderer merely wanted to distract us from his crime."

"And the Bastet statue?" I asked. "When did he steal that?"

"Maybe he quickly smashed the display case in passing and grabbed it to make the break-in look believable, and then hid it in his room? It's risky, though, because the police might search the house." She broke off; her whiskers were vibrating with concentration.

"Never mind," she said then. "What do we care

about the statue? Even if it is dedicated to the great cat goddess, we must not be distracted by a simple theft. We have to solve a murder!"

At this point, Tim and Victoria made a U-turn and started back toward the house. They were no longer talking about the death, but about their future plans. Especially about the history degree that Tim wanted to earn.

For a brief, crazy moment, I wondered if Tim might somehow be persuaded to train as a private detective, rather than enrolling in college. History was a fine thing, but if our humans could better support us in solving the murder cases—in which we were actually involved on a continuous basis, whether we liked it or not—I truly wouldn't mind. Without risking their lives, of course.

I had my paws full, what with bringing two-legged villains to justice and also making sure that Pearl, in her unshakable thirst for action and completely exaggerated self-confidence, did not put her fluffy white neck at risk. That was quite a lot to ask of a single dog!

But I gave up on the pipe dream right away; to influence Tim in this direction would be impossible for me. Human-dog communication was much too rudimentary for that. To make Tim understand that I wanted a cookie?—that was manageable. Let him know that a walk would be a good idea—also no problem. But getting him to rethink his career plans?

That was far beyond my capabilities.

"Athos?" Pearl snapped me out of my thoughts.

"Huh? I'm sorry, did you say something?"

"I said I might know why Tobias couldn't sleep last night and was roaming around the house."

"Oh, yeah?"

"Indeed," she replied, her chest puffed out. "He must have been very upset, because he had a fight with Seschat after dinner."

"I didn't even notice," I said.

"How could you?" Pearl said reprovingly. "After all, you were snoring in the dining room for a good two hours while I was keeping my eyes and ears open."

"Hey!" I protested. "No reason to put on airs just because you were awake for once."

Pearl hissed softly and stomped around the next puddle that blocked her way. I made a point of jumping right over it—extremely elegantly of course, easily overcoming the obstacle.

She marched on in silence without giving me so much as a glance.

I approached her and gave her a conciliatory nudge with my muzzle. "Now tell me, Sherlock—Tobias had a fight with his daughter? What was that all about? You must have listened to every word," I cajoled her. I'm just too nice a dog.

The flattery did not miss its target.

"Sure I did," she replied promptly. "And the heated discussion between Tobias and his daughter was a reaction to another argument, one that took place the day before—between Tobias and Giorgio, Leo's fitness trainer. And, more recently, Seschat's."

I said nothing in reply. Apparently I had also slept through that first argument. At least I hadn't known about it. Did I really take too many naps? But they were vital when you had to take care of two humans and an energetic cat like Pearl. It was a round-the-clock job that was exhausting.

Fortunately I was not to receive any new criticism from the tiny one; Pearl was much too busy telling me about the two-leggeds' quarrels.

"Tobias and Giorgio got into a fight the night before last. Tobias approached him, the two of them went into the garden, presumably so no one could over-hear their conversation—but I followed them, of course—quite inconspicuously."

"Of course," I confirmed reflexively.

"Tobias offered Giorgio money, lots of money, if he would agree to stop training Seschat."

"Excuse me?" I interrupted. "Why is that? He could just forbid his daughter to book any more training sessions, couldn't he? She's only seventeen, after all."

"I was wondering that too," Pearl said. "Well, any-way, Giorgio refused the bribe. He even got pretty mad. *I'm not on the take!* he yelled at Tobias. And then the two of them really went for each other's necks."

"Do you think that could be a motive for murder?" I

thought aloud—only to contradict myself right away. "No, nonsense, you don't kill someone over such a mundane argument."

"Who knows," Pearl said. "The two-leggeds are capable of anything."

"And the fight last night?" I pressed her further. "Between Tobias and Seschat? Was that also about the matter with Giorgio?"

"Exactly. Seschat stormed into her father's study—he was probably going to work for a bit after dinner, but she didn't give a damn. I just managed to sneak in, then she slammed the door behind her. So hard that she almost pinched my tail!" Pearl turned her head to her plush rear end as she walked. The tail twitched indignantly and I had to suppress a sound of amusement.

"Seschat yelled at her father in a total rage. How dare he try to bribe her coach, she threw at him."

"So Giorgio must have told her about the argument the day before," I concluded. "And about her father's financial offer."

"Looks like it. And she was furious about it. She yelled at Tobias: *You know what I'll do if you don't stop treating me like a slave! I'll take you out; I swear to God.*"

"Excuse me?" I said.

"You heard me right. *Slave?* her father yelled back. *You're a teenager, for heaven's sake!* And then Seschat stormed out of the room. This time I didn't even try to follow her." Once again Pearl turned to her tail, which was bobbing along in rhythm with her gait. It looked entirely unscathed to me. There was not a single hair out of place.

"So Seschat threatened her father?" I repeated incredulously. "*I'll take you out*?"

"Sounded quite aggressive to me," Pearl agreed.

Impossible; the idea just wouldn't enter my head. Seschat might be spoiled and pampered, nervewrackingly cool, and perhaps not the most loving daughter one could wish for. But violent?

No, she had certainly not murdered her father—or had his death been an accident after all? Had they had another fight, late at night at the top of the stairs? Whereupon Seschat had given him a shove and he'd fallen to his death?

But this argument would have been overheard, wouldn't it? The girl was a real hothead and got really loud when something went against her grain. And besides, Seschat's shock and her tears when she saw her father lying dead at the foot of the stairs had seemed completely authentic to me.

"Tim and Victoria should know about these quarrels," I said to Pearl.

"They *should*," the midget agreed. "But you know how it is—no way to explain it to the humans. They just aren't intelligent enough for us to have complex conversations with them."

She suddenly stopped and mewed plaintively. Victoria promptly stopped and turned to us with a concerned expression. The next moment she came running and took Pearl in her arms.

The tiny one purred contentedly. "The two-leggeds understand only simple commands, but at least that's better than nothing. And I've really walked far enough for today," she informed me. From her throne on Victoria's arm, she looked down at me like a queen upon her servant.

"My paws have gotten all dirty," she complained.

She would have spent half the day grooming again—if we weren't completely taken up anew by our murder hunt.

6

When we got back to the house the police had returned, in the persons of Melissa Funke and her assistant, Christian Wolf.

They asked Leo, who had only reluctantly taken on the role of master of the house, for permission to use one of the rooms on the ground floor for some conversations with the family and their guests.

He'd let them use the library, a spacious room that, while crammed as expected with bookshelves, also served as another display area for Tobias's Egyptian collection.

If you were to make yourself comfortable on the cozy carpet in the center of the room, you would immediately be stared at from every side by animal-headed figurines, pharaonic statues and even one of the more hideous mummies. In addition, some of the walls were covered with glazed frames sporting papyri emblazoned with paintings and hieroglyphs.

I was a little proud of myself that I had already memorized all these complicated technical terms. But as I've already mentioned, I am a highly educated dog who loves to gain knowledge.

Leo was the first person to be interviewed by Melissa.

"*Interrogations*—that's what they really are, even

though the chief inspector may just call them *conversations*," Pearl opined in a tone of mordant conviction. "Melissa doesn't believe that Tobias suffered an accidental death any more than I do."

I didn't give her an answer. We wandered into the library on Leo's heels—or to be more precise, Leo picked Pearl up from the floor outside in the hallway and carried her into the library, while I stole inconspicuously into the room behind them.

Well, inconspicuously as far as that is possible for a dog of my size. As a splendid almost-wolf you do stand out, and there's nothing you can do about it.

But fortunately no one seemed to object to my presence. Pearl and I often are at a disadvantage in our murder investigations because we are not human detectives, but our gift for eavesdropping on conversations of all kinds without having to hide often proves to be an asset in our favor.

Leo was sweating profusely, but he immediately gave Melissa an explanation.

"Already spent an hour on the ergometer this morning," he announced, "and streamed it live on Facebook. You have to look ahead instead of letting death bring you to your knees. It's a matter of making the most of the life we have left—celebrating it!"

Before Melissa could actually ask him her first question, he pointed to Pearl, who had taken a seat on his lap and was devotedly cleaning her dirty little paws. That is, they were filthy in her eyes only; to me they looked as spotlessly clean as paws could be.

"This little kitty is a real star, a natural in front of the camera," Leo told Melissa. "The husky should be put on a diet, though, if you ask me—but I'll be careful not to mention that to dear Victoria Adler. *Dr. Adler*," he aped her tone of voice. "Typical academic, and a psychologist at that. I'd hate to get on the wrong side of her."

He rolled his eyes.

I was boiling with rage inside. Not only had he insulted my human and mistaken me for a husky, when I was much bigger and stronger—the word *diet* had really set me off.

"He doesn't have a clue," Pearl murmured to me from the unworthy one's lap before I could complain with a loud yelp. "He just doesn't get it about your thick fur! That you're really not that fat."

"What do you mean not *that* fat?" I retorted grumpily. "I'm not fat at all—"

That was as far as I got, because Melissa Funke finally began her questioning, and Pearl and I had to shut up so as not to miss anything.

Her entry into the conversation—or interrogation, if Pearl had her way—was quite unusual. "You told me last night about a curse, Mr. Unruh, one that emanated from the stolen statue ... if I understood you correctly."

"Indeed," confirmed Leo. "You may not believe me, and I am well aware how crazy such a claim may sound in our enlightened age, but I tell you that something evil has emanated from that statue. It has cast a spell over everyone. My son, his friends—even our cat is crazy about the darn thing."

"And the curse," Melissa continued, "how did it manifest itself?"

"How did it manifest itself? It has afflicted us all! No one has been spared. I, for example, have slept badly from the first day Tobias brought the thing into the house. My follower growth has been slower than it was in years, and I—"

"Wait," Melissa interrupted. "Your *follower growth*?" She looked as if she couldn't believe her ears.

Leo, however, nodded as a matter of course. "Don't tell me you're not active on social media? A luddite? I wouldn't have thought so about you. You actually look—"

"Let's get back to my question, please," Melissa interrupted him.

"Alright; the curse. Seschat also has grown ever more obnoxious in the weeks since Tobias took possession of that damn statue. She's behaved like the daughter of a pharaoh, and Tobias let her get away with every bit of her nonsense. Teenagers are known to be particularly susceptible to occult influences, in case you didn't know."

Melissa did not look as if she had ever dealt with this subject before, and Christian Wolf made a face as if he understood nothing at all.

Leo took a short breath, then added: "Of course, women are particularly sensitive and therefore vulnerable to evil, you know. Poor Antonia has truly suffered from Bastet's curse: she has a really depressive disposition, I'm afraid, and it's only gotten worse in recent weeks. That is, strictly speaking, she's actually suffering from mood swings, now that I think about it. Sometimes she can be quite cheerful. I can't really figure out my daughter-in-law, I must admit. Well, in any case, she does suffer from bad nightmares. My bedroom is right next to hers, you see. And sometimes I hear her. Last time..."

He seemed to ponder for a moment. "Yes, it must have been the night before my poor son had his accident that she was terribly unwell again. I heard her gasping and screaming. It wasn't very loud, but I have good ears, you know. And not just for my age. My doctors keep confirming that I have the hearing and also the eyesight of a forty-year-old."

"Impressive," Melissa said, with no real enthusiasm. "So your daughter-in-law sleeps separately from her husband?"

Leo's eyes narrowed. "What kind of question is that? Why would you care?"

Only now did he seem to realize that Melissa probably had in mind a rather extensive investigation of Tobias' death, and was therefore interested in every little detail of its circumstances.

"What the hell are you up to?" Leo demanded of

her. "My son had an accident; I hope you realize that. And you can hardly be intent on arresting Bastet, who is behind it all, with her curse. So what's with all the questions?"

"Just a routine procedure," Melissa assured him with a professional smile. "To get back to your daughter-in-law..."

He waved his hand dismissively. "It's not like it's a secret. Yes, she and Tobias used to sleep separately, but that was only because he snored horribly. Plus, he's got himself a bedroom that looks like one of those damn Egyptian temples. It's in the west wing of the villa, where you have the best view, but I couldn't sleep a wink in that room because the decor makes you think of a tomb all the time. So you really can't blame Antonia for insisting on her own bedroom."

All at once he emitted such a scent-cloud of sorrow and pain that it overcame my nostrils. He began to fondle Pearl's fur, and his fingers seemed shaky and powerless.

"Tobias was most eccentric, indeed," he moaned. "So fanatical in his obsession with Ancient Egypt. He lived only for his collection, and thus not in the present, but three thousand years before our time. The here and now...." He shook his head. "He wasn't the least bit interested in that. His body, for example, he neglected terribly. I never succeeded in encouraging him to exercise regularly—but what does it matter now." His voice died away.

Melissa let a few seconds pass, presumably so he could collect himself a bit, then asked her next question: "How did your son actually acquire the collection? Did he build it all by himself?"

Her gaze wandered around the room, with a mixture of disgust and fascination it seemed to me, only to linger on the mummy in the corner case. The thing was staring at us in kind of an evil way, I thought, although its eyes were not visible of course. Everything was hidden under those bandages that reminded me so much of the humans' toilet paper.

"No, no," Leo said. "Tobias inherited the collection from my brother, Richard, but has expanded it greatly since then."

He suddenly frowned. "The two of them were most alike—Richard and Tobias. Very much so. You'd think Tobias had inherited all his bad qualities from my brother. Sometimes I even wondered if maybe he wasn't *his* son."

He waved his hand again. "Oh, nonsense. But anyway, the Egyptian collection has been in my family for generations. Many of the pieces you find here in the house would be impossible to acquire nowadays, and Tobias often complained that he would have loved to own certain artifacts he had seen in museums, or in his friend Ivo's collection. But it was simply impossible for him to purchase something like that, no matter what price he might have offered for it. All those laws and regulations, you know."

He shrugged his shoulders. "If you want to know more about the collection, you'd best talk to Ivo—or to Julius Feldmann. He was Tobias's most important art dealer. My son used to buy from him regularly."

7

The very next person to be questioned by Melissa was Antonia Unruh. Once again, Christian Wolf was silently crouched in the seat next to her and merely took a few notes, leaving the conversation entirely up to his superior.

Antonia was visibly uncomfortable. She sat so stiffly and rigidly on her chair right from the start that she made me think constantly of the mummy in the corner display case.

I stood up, stretched, and looked for a new place to lie down next to Melissa's chair, so that I would no longer have the hideous thing in front of my eyes, but at the same time I could continue to watch the two-leggeds at the table. Judging by their smell, all three were very tense: Melissa, her assistant, and Antonia especially. But that was only to be expected, given the current circumstances.

Melissa seemed to be very impressed by the curse of the Bastet statue—at least she asked Antonia many questions about it, although she never directly mentioned the word *curse.*

Pearl, who had joined me on the floor, said, "It makes sense that Melissa would be interested in the statue. After all, Bastet *was* stolen, and maybe she was the actual motive for the murder. Which is not to say that the goddess couldn't have cursed the humans as well," she quickly added. "She may not have wanted her statue removed from the temple or tomb where it originally stood."

"I think the Unruhs' villa is in no way inferior to a temple," I said. But what did I know about cat goddesses and their preferences? I already had enough trouble trying to figure out Pearl's everyday whims and vagaries.

"In your opinion, was there any change after the purchase of the Bastet statue?" Melissa asked Antonia. "In your husband's life, or in his behavior, perhaps?"

"No." Antonia furrowed her brow. "What are you getting at?"

When she didn't get an answer right away, she continued, "Tobias loved that statue, if that's what you mean. Even our cat adored it—she would often sit in front of it and stare at the thing, just like a person looking at a beloved work of art. Tobias always thought it was so droll." She smiled sadly. "She's called Bastet, too, you know—our cat. Tobias was crazy about her."

"And other than that?" Melissa persisted. "Have you noticed any changes in the other residents of the house lately? In your daughter, perhaps, or in yourself?"

"Because of the statue?" The wrinkles on Antonia's forehead deepened. "Definitely not. What are you getting at, anyway?"

Again, Melissa failed to answer her and instead simply asked her the next question: "Can you think of any reason why someone would want to harm your husband? Did he make any enemies? Or have a fight with someone?"

"*Enemies?*" Antonia repeated in a strained voice. "So you don't think he was killed by that ... intruder? By the burglar who stole the statue?"

"These are just some routine questions, Mrs. Un-ruh," Melissa reassured her. "We have to consider all the possibilities at this early stage of the investigation, that's all."

Antonia nodded slowly, but didn't look completely convinced.

"Didn't you hear anything last night when your husband fell down the stairs?" Melissa continued, unperturbed.

"No. I sleep upstairs on the first floor, you know, and my room is quite far from the stairwell."

"And do you have any idea why your husband was still up at such a late hour?"

"I thought it was the burglar who woke him up?"

"That's possible, but rather unlikely," Melissa replied. "If a window shatters downstairs in the dining room, you certainly wouldn't hear it in his bedroom. That's quite a distance from the stairwell, isn't it?"

• Antonia nodded reflexively. "Yes, you're right."

She put on a brooding expression, and Melissa

60

looked at her inquiringly, but for now did not ask anything further.

Finally Antonia said, perhaps because she was uncomfortable with the resulting silence: "Tobias almost never slept through the night—he often wandered around the house at a very late hour. Sometimes he went downstairs to the kitchen to get a glass of milk, and we would meet there occasionally. I'm also drawn to the refrigerator when I can't sleep." There it was again, the sad smile flitting across Antonia's pale features like a delicate butterfly.

"*Milk*?" repeated Melissa.

Antonia nodded, putting on another wistful expression. "I asked Tobias about it once, when we were newlyweds. It was probably a childhood memory of his: milk was his mother's home remedy for her little boy's insomnia, and so he kept resorting to it as a grown man. Instead of, say, indulging in a whiskey."

The policewoman's next question came unexpectedly, and as if shot from a pistol—which may have been intentional. "How would you describe your marriage, Mrs. Unruh? Were the two of you happy together?"

"Oh yes. Everything was perfect," Antonia answered, far too quickly and with too much emphasis. It was as if she first had to convince herself of the truth of her words.

"One last question and we'll be done," Melissa said. "Did your husband leave a will?"

"Yes, of course. Seschat and I will each inherit certain assets, and I'll manage her share until her eighteenth birthday."

"And she's seventeen now, isn't she?"

Antonia nodded wordlessly.

"It's a very large fortune, I take it?" the policewoman probed further. "Can you give me a rough estimate?"

Antonia pulled up her shoulders. "I really don't know exactly. The villa, the collection—my husband also owned some investment properties, apartment buildings in Vienna—and securities, of course. I'm sorry, but I've never dealt with any of that. It must be a few hundred million euros in total."

Melissa's eyebrows arched upwards. She didn't comment, though, only glancing at her colleague, who was jotting down Antonia's estimate on his pad.

Ivo Lindquist, Tobias's friend and an historian and fellow Egyptian antiquities collector, was shown into the library next.

He looked over the exhibits—which he certainly already knew in detail—without any disgust, but on the contrary, seemed downright fascinated at the sight of them. And that included the toilet paper guy in the corner display case.

But Ivo didn't really have anything interesting to tell the two police detectives.

"Your guest room is closest to the foot of the stairs," Melissa noted. "How come you didn't hear anything of your friend's fatal fall? He may not have cried out, but surely the fall itself must have caused some noise."

Ivo gave her a suspicious look, but then answered readily. "That's easily explained, dear Chief Inspector. I am a very light sleeper, and that's why I always use earplugs. It's an old habit of mine."

He gave me a scrutinizing look, only to make himself persona non grata with me again with his next words.

"It was the howling of that dog that brought me out of my sleep. It was as loud as an alarm siren. I jumped out of bed, ran to the door and then the few steps down the corridor to the entry hall. Where I found my poor friend—dead." He screwed up his face. "Oh God, at first I thought that mutt had attacked Tobias!"

I received another very unfriendly look, which I returned with a low growl.

Then, addressing Melissa again, Ivo added, "I really don't understand why people keep working dogs from Arctic climes in our latitudes in the twenty-first century." He shrugged and grinned stupidly.

I forced myself to remain calm, but this man had moved up several spots on my list of suspects all at once.

He had called me a *mutt*. What a bully! It is true, of course, that I am a working dog from Arctic climes, but from his mouth it had sounded like an insult as well.

Pearl licked my muzzle comfortingly after Ivo's question session was over and the unsympathetic moron had left the room. Melissa took a smoke break on the terrace in front of the library, while Christian stayed in the room and made a phone call on his cell.

"Any news from our Doctor Death?" Melissa asked him after she had returned from the garden. I assumed that this nickname must refer to the medical examiner.

"Cause of death has not yet been determined," Christian said curtly. "But as for the time: our victim must have died right before his body was found—five to ten minutes earlier, at most."

"Hmm, okay. Too bad; that doesn't get us anywhere. Everyone in the house claims to have been sound asleep—before this husky here started howling, and Mr. Lindquist then called for help. And everyone was sleeping alone, except for this Dr. Adler and her boyfriend. But those two had only known our victim for a short time, so I really can't make out any possible motive."

"Me neither," Christian said with a frown.

"Let's get on with it," Melissa said decidedly, and next the two tackled Julius Feldmann, the art dealer.

He had not been asleep at the time of Tobias's death and could even offer an alibi—or at least that's what he claimed.

"I was on a video call with a client in Sydney," he stated baldly. "Not a great time of day for me, but you have to accommodate your client. Their time zone, that is. We were in the middle of a price negotiation when I heard a scream from the hall: a call for help from Mr. Lindquist, as I later learned."

"Your guest room is located on the ground floor, a little further from the hall than the one occupied by Mr. Lindquist," Christian Wolf spoke up. It was not a question, but a statement that he'd taken from his notes.

Feldmann acknowledged with a curt nod of his head.

"You didn't hear the dog howl before Mr. Lindquist raised the alarm?" asked Melissa.

"That's possible; I really wasn't paying attention. It was only when I heard the scream, in the middle of the night, that it caught my attention. The thick old walls here in the villa muffle every sound, you know. The nights before, I didn't hear a thing—the silence was almost eerie. And even Mr. Lindquist's scream didn't really reach me loudly at all. But I did hear it, and it was clear to me that it was not coming from a TV set. Somehow I had the feeling that something was off, I can't explain it any better than that. So I told my client that I would get back to him later, quickly put on my robe and went to investigate what was going on in the hall. My client will be happy to confirm my statement, I'm sure. And the exact time of our video call can certainly be gleaned from my computer. You are welcome to check it out at any time."

Very obliging, went through my head. Was that a good sign or a bad one?

8

The Unruhs' two-legged guests had obeyed Melissa Funke's request and had all remained in the house. Julius Feldmann had grumbled that urgent business awaited him in Vienna, but no one had paid any attention to his complaints—so he'd finally joined everyone else at the large table on the dining room's terrace, where a late dinner was being served.

The patio door's broken glass pane had not yet been replaced, but at least the room and the terrace had already been released for use again by the police.

The weather was glorious for an outdoor garden dinner. The sun was just setting as a glowing fireball behind the treetops, crickets were chirping in the grass, Pearl had devoted herself to her grooming, and our two humans were having an aperitif together with the other two-leggeds. As is well known, the humans like to make elaborate rituals out of their drinking habits—before the meal, with the meal, after the meal. There are always different glasses and different forms of alcohol, none of which particularly appeal to this dog's nose.

As expected, the mood at the table was rather subdued: little was said, and a lot was drunk.

Leo's fitness trainer, Giorgio, was eating with us. He didn't talk much at first either, occasionally glancing over at Seschat and then at Antonia, but eventually he started a forced conversation with Leo about weight training. That's another quirk of the two-leggeds that I'll probably never understand; they do *sports*. That is to say, they wear themselves out when there is no necessity for it whatsoever. Such behavior would never occur to a dog, or any other animal—our kind runs and jumps and hops when it is needed, but otherwise we rest.

Luisa, the Unruhs' Portuguese housekeeper, served dinner with a tearful expression. Apparently she'd been very fond of her employer, and was struggling to cope with his death.

Luisa wore her dark hair long, including a fringe on her forehead that kept falling into her face. She reminded me a bit of those unfortunate bobtail dogs that have such a head of hair that they are as good as blind.

The Unruhs only had this single employee who lived in the house; quite a modest staff compared to other houses where Pearl and I had been guests and had also solved murders.

Damn, it was really disturbing, this matter of all these two-leggeds losing their lives wherever we went. Maybe there really was a curse on Pearl and me, similar to the one that seemed to be emanating from the Bastet statue. We brought death....

I stood up, spun around in a circle twice, and settled back down in a more comfortable position. The terrace was covered with pleasant-smelling wooden planks, which didn't cool your belly as well as stone did, but they were a bit softer to lie on.

No, we do not bring death, I decided. Pearl and I hadn't been responsible for all of the two-leggeds who had died. On the contrary, we'd lent a helping paw in catching their murderers, and we would do the same again this time—even though I still had no idea how we were going to achieve it, or if there even truly was a killer in this house.

I was seized with a thirst for action.

"Come on, come on," I said to Pearl, who had just scrounged a piece of grilled fish from Victoria. "We have to do something!"

"Do what?" Pearl asked with her mouth full. "Don't stress, Fatt— uh, Athos!"

"Don't be so gluttonous," I said in retaliation for her almost insulting me again. "I want to ask the animals here in the garden whether they didn't see anything at the time Tobias died and this patio door was smashed. Or at least whether they heard something. If there was no real burglar, then this Bastet statue must still be around here somewhere. And the house has already been searched by Melissa and her team."

"The garden, too," Pearl said, still smacking her lips.

She put on her *I'm-the-most-hungry-kitten-in-the-world* look, peering up at Victoria, but no more fish was forthcoming.

She licked her lips in disgruntlement. "The staff isn't

quite what it used to be," she grumbled. "Is Victoria trying to starve me or what?"

I refrained from uttering the comment that was on the tip of my tongue—namely that she could easily fast for two weeks without running any risk of starvation.

Instead, I focused on our case.

"The police have only done a cursory sweep of the garden," I said. "It's way too big and too inaccessible in some places for a handful of two-leggeds to really search it thoroughly. Let's ask around to see if any of the wild quadrupeds or birds didn't witness something. If we can find the statue, maybe we can make some progress with our murder investigation."

This worked; I knew by now how to lure Pearl. Food of course came first with her, and that would never change. This was closely followed by the proper care of her fur. But third of all—after the glutton and the diva—Pearl was a most passionate detective. So she forgot to be angry with Victoria for not serving her enough fish, got up onto her paws and joined me.

"Where do we start? Who should we ask?" She looked around the park, also seized by a sudden urge to act.

"Preferably around here, near the patio door," I replied. "The animals whose territory this is, are the most likely to have observed something."

No sooner said than done; we stomped off. That is, I strolled comfortably while Pearl bounced wildly to keep up with me. If I had also galloped along, we would have driven away the entire fauna of the garden in one fell swoop—because when I sprint towards someone, I look pretty scary for sure.

So I took it slow, but unfortunately we found that numerous birds nevertheless took off from their branches and twigs and took flight with alarmed chirping. Most of the small terrestrial animals in the park reacted in a similar way.

"Maybe I should look for a witness on my own?" suggested Pearl.

"One who'd devour you right away because you don't have a protector with you? Out of the question!"

Pearl emitted a sound that could only be described as a grunt, and which wasn't particularly feline.

We carefully forged ahead, with me almost crawling on my stomach. What kind of wimps were living here in the park of this villa? Was it because such a high fence protected the estate, and they were used to living in an island of the meek and peaceful—far from the evils of the wider world?

Anyway, we had to roam around for quite a while before we finally found our key witness.

9

The witness in question was a bat: a rather small, jet-black specimen that was hanging upside down on a sturdy branch and seemed to be dozing off.

She was alone—rather atypical for a bat—and when she caught sight of me, her wings only twitched briefly, but otherwise she remained unmoved. Remarkable; what a daredevil flapper.

I immediately addressed her before she could change her mind, asking her about the night hours in which Tobias Unruh had lost his life. Bats are known to be nocturnal, so it was a good fit.

Pearl, however, whispered to me, "What's that supposed to do for us? These fluttery critters can't see properly, they just have that echolocation thingy."

"I can see *you* quite clearly thanks to my echolocation 'thingy,' you arrogant cat gnome," the bat shot back, before I could silence Pearl.

That hit home. Pearl let out a startled meow—which doesn't happen very often. Normally she is not easily intimidated.

Ruefully, she apologized to the bat for her prejudices. Which saved us; otherwise the black flapper would hardly have helped us out.

The bats' unique echolocation system is based on very fast and high-pitched sounds, which they emit to orient themselves by means of the echo, and which I can hear, unlike the comparatively deaf two-leggeds. In addition, they are damn fast flyers, even if you would not believe it judging by their rather puny-looking wings of skin and bone.

I told our potential witness that we were looking for a burglar, for a two-legged who had entered the villa the night before last and broken a pane of glass. Or perhaps for someone who had stepped out of the house onto the terrace to break the pane from there.

"Were you able to locate a person in the park, perhaps?" I asked the bat. "A few hours before sunrise? And then did you register the clinking of the shattering glass?" Our flapper with her sonar might have detected that, too, after all.

I tilted my head, almost dislocating it, because I somehow felt the polite need to see my conversation partner upright in front of me, but the bat was still dangling upside down from its branch. I couldn't explain how it managed not to get a headache.

The bat seemed to ponder for a while—while I wondered how good the memory of these animals might honestly be. I must admit that I'd had little to do with these nocturnal flutterers up to that point. But a good detective does not exclude any possible witness.

"Tell you what," she finally said, "I happened to be here the night you're talking about, quite close to that pane of glass that shattered ... or rather that was smashed. Although I can hear, and therefore see, across the entire garden, if need be; my sonar reaches very far, probably farther than your eyes." This statement was clearly a small rebuke directed at Pearl. "But the person who smashed the window was certainly not a burglar, I think."

"Why not?" asked Pearl—in a decidedly more polite tone.

"Well, burglars break in, don't they?" replied the bat, a little precociously. "But this two-legged left the house through the patio door, came running a little way into the garden, and threw away something that had the outline of a member of your species. It wasn't a living cat, though, because it was stiff as a board and its skin was made of something that sounded quite like metal. After that, the two-legged quickly ran back into the house—and only then, on his way back, did he break the glass door."

"So the break-in *was* a fake," Pearl exclaimed. "Just as we suspected, Athos!"

Indeed! I was panting with excitement. We had found exactly the right witness ... but now I had to ask her a question that was a bit tricky, because it was once again questioning her eyesight, or at least the capabilities of her sonar.

"Were you able to see *who* it was that was leaving the house?" I asked her.

"What do you mean, who?" the flapper replied. "A biped, usual size. Not fat or anything, nor a child

74

either. They were moving quickly, so probably not an old person."

"Man or woman?" I asked.

"I don't know. I wasn't paying much attention, you see. I was actually just getting some rest. I'd been hunting and needed to take a break." She spread her membranous wings and then closed them again. My neck was hurting badly by now, so I gave up trying to look at her the right way around.

"But you must have seen *where* the two-legged threw away the metal cat, right?" I asked hopefully.

"Of course. He ran to the thicket where the tasty moths live," replied the bat. "And he threw the stiff cat in there."

"Um, yeah ... and where is that, please?" Tasty moths were definitely not on *my* menu.

The bat detached itself from its branch and fluttered away.

"What's the matter, aren't you coming?" she chirped when we didn't run after her right away. "It's right over here."

She flew toward a thicket that lay perhaps twenty dog-lengths from the dining room, but which looked like a patch of utter wilderness. In general, the Unruhs didn't seem to be overly obsessed with a perfectly manicured garden. The lawn looked as if it was mowed occasionally, but otherwise everything here looked quite natural, not to say even rather overgrown.

The bat landed on the branch of one of the trees growing within the thicket, and promptly dangled upside down again. I forced myself to keep my aching neck straight. Slowly I was getting used to the fact that our witness had her feet up and her nose down.

"Here in these bushes—she must be hidden here somewhere, the stiff cat you are looking for. That's where the human threw her in." She emitted her high-pitched sounds again, which went right into my bones thanks to my fine hearing, but then she apologized: "Sorry, I can't find the cat; the bushes are too thick for me. So many leaves, undergrowth, and branches. Moving targets are more my thing, you know. I'm afraid you'll have to find the metal cat yourself if you want it—I can't imagine you can eat it, though."

And with that, she fluttered away. "Pet animals are so strange," she mused to herself as she disappeared into the twilight.

I called out a *thank you* after her, and she responded with a new wave of her shrill clicking sounds. Presumably she was already on the lookout for the next tasty moth.

"We're supposed to go in *there*?" Pearl said indignantly, eyeing the thicket. "She can't be serious." She excitedly licked one of her paws, probably already fretting that her silky fur might be damaged.

What a softie of a sofa-loving cat.

Of course, I was not discouraged by such snivellings, but instead looked for a place where I could best penetrate the thicket.

Right at the edge of the undergrowth, a mass of hideous burdock bushes grew, and stretched out to grab me on the gravel path that led past them. But what the hell ... a fearless malamute like me can handle such monsters!

I made my way into the undergrowth, sniffed—and was bombarded by a hundred different smells. Most of them came from plants, or from insects. From rodents, toads....

Fortunately, my dense fur saved me from getting too many painful scratches, only my poor muzzle was hurt quite a bit when I had to squeeze through here and there. Pearl with her small size would definitely have had it easier in here, but of course Madame's fluffy fur could not be put at risk.

I searched further—until I finally sniffed something that smelled faintly of the two-leggeds. It had to be the statue!

I followed my nose, caught another dozen burrs in my fur, but finally found the stiff cat, as our bat-witness had dubbed it. Bastet was unharmed; bronze seems to be a fairly indestructible material.

I called out to Pearl: "I have found Bastet! What are we going to do now? Should we direct Victoria or Tim in here? You know what an important role the location of evidence always plays in mystery novels."

"You're going to lure them into that jungle?" cried

Pearl, startled. "No way!"

She was not entirely wrong. There was no way through here for our two-leggeds. No wonder Melissa Funke's police team had not found the statue.

"Can't you bring it out?" Pearl suggested. "Or is it too heavy for you?"

"*Too heavy*?" I grumbled.

What did she think I was, a weakling? I could easily take the thing in my mouth and carry it back to Pearl, to the gravel path, where the two-leggeds had easy access. The way back through the thicket wasn't long at all—I had just walked in circles forever in my search.

I thought hard. Was there any way to show the two-leggeds where I had discovered the statue? Was the place of discovery even important to our case?

Obviously, the criminal who had stolen the statue had simply hurled it into the thicket from the gravel path, which must mean that he had not really wanted to steal it. He had only nicked Bastet to fake a burglary, and then had simply run from the dining room into the garden, towards the nearest thicket.

Otherwise he would hardly have thrown the statue into this little jungle, where he would never find it again. And also that had to mean that this person, by committing the theft, had only wanted to distract from Tobias's death—which therefore could not have been an accident.

My skull was humming. I sniffed the statue. Yes, it

smelled of human. Especially of Tobias, but that was no surprise.

Who had stolen the statue, and then thrown it into the undergrowth, I could not determine with the help of my nose.

How annoying.

I opened my muzzle wide, grabbed Bastet as gently as I could, and then made my way back to the gravel path where Pearl was waiting for me.

From here it was only a short distance to the dining table of the two-leggeds. Fortunately they were still sitting there, drinking their foul-smelling alcohol, and also some coffee that didn't give off such a bad odor.

Pearl and I rushed towards our humans, yelping, meowing, yapping ... the usual protocol, which by now didn't take long to achieve its desired effect.

Victoria and Tim jumped up, apologized embarrassedly to the other two-leggeds, who were rather frightened by my wild barking and Pearl's cat-song, and followed us without hesitation to the thistle thicket. On the gravel path in front of it they discovered Bastet, which I had left there for them to find.

They were beside themselves with excitement. "Oh, wow, you found the statue! You're so amazing. Where was it?"

I took a step closer to the thistle thicket to point out where I had found it, but took pains not to catch any more of the pesky burrs. My fur was peppered with them.

Tim noticed this, carefully pulling one of the monsters out of my fur, and then stared down at the insidious plants.

In the next instant, he clapped his right hand onto his bare left arm. "Damn!"

"What's wrong?" Victoria asked in alarm.

"Oh, just a gnat that has stung me. I hate these little beasts!" He looked down at his palm, which was empty. There was no corpse of a biting insect to be seen. "And I missed it, too," he grumbled.

"There's a little pond right over there," Victoria said, pointing her hand over Tim's shoulder and then making a face herself. "Just the right breeding ground for these pests. It's a wonder, really, that we were left relatively alone on the terrace."

"There are those mosquito candles on the table," Tim said, "and now I know why."

"Ouch!" Victoria bent down, checking her legs. "Damn, they've got me too. But that's not important right now!" Our two-leggeds refocused themselves on us and our heroic deed. The mosquitoes couldn't steal our thunder.

Pearl was petted, my head was cuddled and more burrs were removed from my fur, then Tim resolutely pulled out his cell phone and called Melissa Funke.

"The statue—Bastet. We've found it!" he reported breathlessly. "Well, actually, it was our pets who found it."

Honor to whom honor is due. I gave Tim's leg an appreciative nudge with my nose.

10

Tim hung up and turned to Victoria. "Ms. Funke and her team will be here in about an hour. We're not supposed to touch anything in the meantime."

He had given Melissa a rather vague explanation over the phone as to how and why the statue had suddenly been retrieved. "Apparently our pets picked it up somewhere and carried it to the path. It certainly wasn't in this spot before, or your team could hardly have missed it."

He bent down and picked up Pearl, who had just settled down in front of the cat goddess and was looking at the idol as though smitten with it.

"I think Pearl would like a statue like that, too," Victoria joked. "The fact that the ancient Egyptians worshipped her kind probably appeals to our little diva."

Tim grinned. "Looks like it."

He patted Pearl's head, but then he committed an unforgivable sacrilege. He said to the tiny one, "You know, Pearl, I don't want to rob you of your illusions, but the ancient Egyptians didn't really worship animals. They only gave their gods animal heads to symbolize certain qualities that they admired and attributed to the immortals. Just as we still talk about the courage of a lion, for example—or of the cunning of a fox."

"Oh really?" said Victoria. "I was under the impression that cats were practically sacred back then."

Tim shook his head. "In Christianity, for example, we call Jesus the Lamb of God because he sacrificed himself for our sins. But that doesn't mean we worship lambs because of that; on the contrary, we kill them for our Easter feasts."

"I hope you're not going to claim that the ancient Egyptians ate cats," Victoria said, startled.

Pearl jumped from Tim's arms back onto the ground, wearing a distraught expression.

"Not quite that," Tim said quickly. "But they did something you'd rather not think about either: they offered mummified cats as sacrifices to the gods, and I'm afraid those animals didn't die of natural causes. Archaeologists have found so many cat mummies that one must assume a regular breeding scheme to satisfy the demand. Therefore you really can't claim that cats—that is, the living animals—were sacred to the Egyptians, unfortunately."

"You're well on your way to becoming a historian," Victoria said with an appreciative smile.

He waved it off. "Oh, I heard that from Ivo, but it seemed interesting to me, even if it shocked our poor little Pearl. Am I imagining it, or does she look like she's pouting? Almost as if she understood everything I've said."

"Ow!" he shouted the next moment. He lashed out again with the flat of his hand, this time hitting his neck. "Damn these gnats!"

"What are we supposed to do about the statue now?" asked Victoria. "Until Ms. Funke arrives—stay here and keep an eye on the thing?"

"Then these dreadful mosquitoes will eat us alive," Tim said.

"But we can't just leave the statue here, can we?" Victoria looked uncertain. "Completely unguarded?"

Tim looked toward the house. "Nobody knows she's here, right?"

"We are very close to the terrace where we all had dinner," Victoria continued to protest. "If anyone wanted to stretch their feet a bit.... Besides, didn't everyone take note of how our animals came rushing up and we ran off with them? Someone might want to check on us." She looked around like a spy on a top-secret mission.

I sat down on my hind paws next to the statue, straightened my back, let my tongue hang out of my mouth and panted encouragingly.

I have the situation completely under control, I signaled to my humans. *I will guard the statue. You can count on me.*

These poor effeminate people without fur. They fly to the moon, but a swarm of gnats can chase them off.

Victoria understood immediately. "Oh, great idea, Athos! Good dog!" She patted my head; I also received a few appreciative words from Tim, and in the next moment the two gnat victims had already sought shelter in the distance.

"Humans," said Pearl. "Sometimes they're real sissies. And as for Tim, he's got a lot to learn if he wants to be a historian. He must have misunderstood about the cats in ancient Egypt; it can't be true."

"Certainly not," I agreed with her, so as not to offend the poor pipsqueak even more.

She accepted this without further comment, then approached me and began to devote herself to cleaning my fur. She picked out the burrs that Tim had overlooked—of which there were still quite a few. The beastly things had clawed at me by the dozens during my mission in the undergrowth, but they could no more harm me than any mosquitoes could. Although I must say that Pearl's cleaning impulse was most convenient for me.

Half an eternity passed until Pearl let go of me and sat down on her hind paws. However, of Melissa and her team there was still no sign. So maybe only half an hour had passed?

Pearl, at any rate, was exhausted. She gagged and spat, probably because some of the tiny burdock hairs had gotten stuck in her snout and even on her tongue.

"Disgusting things," she complained. "I have to go to the water bowl for a minute—be right back."

And with that she strutted off, bushy tail raised, down the gravel path toward the house.

Sometimes my little diva can be quite brave. And of course, hopeless softie that I am, I was warmed by the thought that she had fought with these nasty burrs for my sake.

Suddenly a thought came to me—*burrs*. Hadn't I already seen the things somewhere, just a few days ago? Not here in the garden ... no, it had been in the house.

I panted to cool myself down a bit, and then it came back to me. Of course! I had noticed the burrs on a trouser leg, the very night that Tobias had fallen down the stairs and I had raised the alarm. One of the humans who had come running into the hall in the aftermath had had a burr on his pants.

I had not paid further attention to it, given the fact that a man lay dead in the hall, but now I realized that this observation had been important. The wearer of the pants had perhaps been out here, right where I was now sitting at the edge of a thistle thicket, to make the Bastet statue disappear into the undergrowth. For whatever reason. And in the process he had caught a burr. Until now, this thicket was the first and only place in the Unruhs' park where I had found the clinging nuisances.

Only, who had been the wearer of the pants in question? A man, a woman? What kind of pants had I seen? They were made of a dark fabric, I thought I remembered. Wool?

I tried to recall what each of the two-leggeds had

worn that night when they appeared in the hall. But all I could remember was that Antonia had shown up in a nightgown. Everyone else ... I couldn't say for the life of me, no matter how hard I panted. *What a bummer.*

Before I could ponder further, I was distracted by the rustling of leaves. I got onto my paws—because in the meantime I had given up the perfect watchdog pose and made myself comfortable next to Bastet. Within a few moments, however, I was standing there with pricked ears, listening hard.

Then I saw them: first Seschat, who was quickly moving away from the house and heading for an area of the garden to my left, immediately followed by Giorgio, Leo's fitness trainer.

As soon as they were out of sight of the house—but still in my field of vision—Seschat stopped, turned to Giorgio and threw her arms around his neck.

An astonished yelp escaped me—which the two fortunately didn't hear. They were too fixated on each other.

She wanted to kiss him, but he hesitated. He held her in his muscular arms, then pushed her a little bit away from him so that he could look into her face.

"How are you doing, sweetie?" he asked with genuine concern in his voice. "Are you going to be okay?"

She screwed up her face. That was clearly not what she'd wanted to hear. Nevertheless, she finally gave an answer. "Yes—no! He was my father, damn it.

Even if he did, well, get on my nerves more often than not. I just can't believe he's gone. Forever."

Suddenly she sobbed, "I'm going to miss him!" And with that she snuggled into Giorgio's arms.

This time he allowed the tenderness, even hugged her tightly and stroked her hair to comfort her.

When she lifted her head again and her lips approached his, I saw him hesitate once more. But then he kissed her—and very passionately too.

After a little while she broke away from him, grinned and grabbed his hand. "At least now my father can no longer come between us. Let's go, this way! I know a really great place. You'll love it."

"You're only seventeen, Seschat," Giorgio protested, though not very forcefully. "We really shouldn't—"

"What nonsense!" she interrupted him. "I'm not a toddler anymore. Just look at me." She stretched her back, and his gaze went right where she wanted it: to her breasts.

"I've had guys who were older than you," she claimed, "and they told me I was really great at ... *you know*." She kissed him again.

This time his resistance was even weaker, even shorter. For a moment he braced himself against her, but then he let himself be pulled along—indeed, he literally ran after her. Like Pearl would have done after a wriggling salmon.

I heard the two still giggling, but then they disappeared from my field of vision. They ran deeper into the garden, and what they were up to there, even a dog such as I could imagine all too well.

I dropped back onto my stomach. The bronze cat goddess stared at me: wordlessly, knowingly. It was kind of creepy.

"Are you really a goddess?" I asked her, half expecting a voice deep from within the shining body of the statue to give me an answer. But that, of course, didn't happen.

11

Whatever has happened to Melissa Funke and her team, I asked myself. Shouldn't they be here by now? Too bad that when you're a dog, you don't have a wristwatch. Or one of those cell phones that also tell you the time.

Suddenly there was a rustling again, this time behind me. Again I jumped up. A person had come running across the lawn, directly toward me.

It was Julius Feldmann, the art dealer.

He was—or only pretended to be?—amazed to see me and the cat goddess. "Oh my gosh, Athos, what have you got there? Why, that's the stolen statue. I'd better take it!"

He wanted to reach for the cat, but I gave him a growl to warn him to keep his hands off it.

Startled, he jerked his hand back. "Athos! What are you doing! You wouldn't bite me, would you?"

Yes, I would, I signaled to him with raised lips. I was on duty after all, if not as a police dog, then at least on an official mission.

He took a step back and I thought I had scared him away. I assumed that he would run back to the house to tell my humans about the find of the statue. He couldn't know that Tim and Victoria—and even Melissa Funke—had been informed long ago.

I had already let myself sink back onto my stomach and did not pay attention to the man's next movement; an unforgivable mistake.

His hand suddenly sprang forward. He grabbed the statue before I could even growl, let alone bare my teeth—and the next moment he lashed out. He had unceremoniously turned the bronze cat goddess into his weapon.

I saw the thing come hurtling toward me, felt the draft of air ... then a ghastly pain drove through my skull.

Everything went black.

When I came to, my head was pounding. Something was tickling my nose and had made it wet.

Pearl! She was sitting right in front of me, and was devotedly licking my muzzle.

"Phew, you're alive! So lucky. I thought..."

She did not continue any further. "What happened?" she wanted to know instead.

Behind her, a group of two-leggeds was approaching. The image blurred before my eyes; I tried to get up on my paws, but staggered like a biped who had drunk too much. I stopped and forced myself to sit down again.

The people coming toward us were Tim, Victoria, Melissa, and two other police officers.

I had failed as a guard. The statue had been stolen

from me, and I knew by whom! Julius Feldmann.

There was no trace of the villain—of course. Surely he had made off with his loot after the brazen attack on me.

The humans reached us, and while Victoria noticed that something was wrong with me, Tim immediately registered that the statue was gone.

I whimpered with shame because I had failed so miserably. My humans had officially assigned me to guard duty, and I had let myself be beaten like a rank beginner.

Instead of wallowing in self-pity, however, I pressed my nose to the ground and began to sniff around. Julius Feldmann mustn't get away with this outrage! I had to let the humans know that he was the villain they were looking for.

I managed to pick up his trail, even though I still felt very dazed. I followed the scent, running towards the villa. That is, perhaps I waddled rather than ran, but I didn't care. I could recover later, when this scoundrel and animal abuser was behind bars.

He had walked along near the villa's facade, that was very clear to me. I continued to follow the trail. My skull felt as if it might explode at any moment.

Pearl ran after me, and managed to catch up with a wild sprint, while the bipeds still lagged behind a bit. But at least I registered with satisfaction that they were also following me.

"Who was it?" Pearl asked breathlessly. "Who are

we looking for?"

"Feldmann! He knocked me down and grabbed the statue."

"The insolence!" hissed Pearl. Then she pressed her snub nose to the ground as well, sniffing and running close to my side as if she were *my* bodyguard.

Cats do have a useful sense of smell, even if it's not nearly as well developed as ours. But now was not the time for such competitive thinking; we had to catch Feldmann.

The trail led to the parking lot in front of the villa—and to an empty parking space. I could still perceive exhaust fumes, though, which must mean that Feldmann had taken off by car.

The two-leggeds reached us a few moments later. Melissa looked around the parking lot and eyed the cars that were still there.

Tim gave her a hint, pointing to the empty parking space where Pearl and I had come to a stop. "Julius Feldmann's car was parked here," he said without hesitation. "A dark blue Jaguar sedan."

12

Melissa Funke assured us that she would find Julius Feldmann. "You can't go into hiding all that easily if you're not a professional criminal," she said with confidence.

"Would you let us know as soon as he's caught?" Tim asked her. "I'm an ... uh, aspiring historian, and I'm really interested to know what the statue is all about. I want to find out why it's so valuable that he would want to steal it, when he himself had been the one to sell it to Tobias Unruh in the first place. And most importantly, what is it about this cat goddess that he was willing to commit murder for it?"

He looked at Melissa searchingly. When she didn't answer, he added, "He did murder Tobias, didn't he, even though he claims to have an alibi? He told us he made a video call to a client in Australia, but he might have—"

"You'll be hearing from me, Mr. Mortensen," Melissa said curtly, cutting him off. Apparently, she didn't want to reveal any details of her investigation. And a few minutes later, she and her team had already disappeared.

"*Aspiring historian,*" Victoria said with a smile when we were back amongst ourselves. She stood on her tiptoes and kissed Tim. "And a sleuth, huh?" she added. "A wonderful combination, I think."

He grinned. "I couldn't agree more." He pulled her close, kissed her again, then asked, "Don't you agree—that Julius must be guilty?"

Victoria shrugged indecisively. "But why? I don't understand about the statue either ... why first sell it to Tobias and afterwards steal it again? That doesn't make any sense. You don't commit murder just to be able to sell some art object twice."

"Maybe it's not just any art object," Tim said thoughtfully. "You know what I'm going to do, first thing in the morning? I'm going to grab Ivo—he's, um, a much more advanced historian than I am. And we'll do some research on this statue, anything we can find out about it. Maybe we'll see a bit clearer after that."

"Good plan. I think I'll have a little chat with Luisa in the meantime, then."

"The housekeeper?"

Victoria nodded. "The perfect source of information if you want to know what goes on behind the scenes in a mansion." She grinned. "I'm hoping she's not averse to gossip."

The two were very pleased with themselves. Then, at last, they remembered that I had been wounded in my guard dog service and took me to a veterinary clinic that was open for night duty.

There I was groped, scrutinized, x-rayed and exam-ined with all kinds of equipment by a lady doctor who smelled unpleasantly of chemicals but was very friendly. Several times I had to walk up and down the room and finally I was fed a sausage into which the doctor had smuggled a pill with a disgusting taste.

In the end, she announced to Tim, "Your dog is fine. All he suffered was a mild concussion. His thick fur probably saved him from worse."

Finally someone had said that! My thick fur was good for something after all, and not just for ruining my figure.

The doctor added, this time turning to Victoria, "I gave Athos something for the pain. You should feed him another tablet tomorrow, too, so he doesn't suffer at all." She handed her a packet of pills. "He'll be back to his old self in a day or two," she added confidently.

As a farewell I got another piece of sausage without a foul-tasting tablet in it, and was then received by Pearl, who had been waiting in the car, like a homecoming hero. I enjoyed that very much, but of course I did not let her notice.

The next morning, Tim and Victoria put their plans into action. Tim convinced Ivo to do some research with him on the Bastet statue, while Victoria directed her steps to the kitchen, where the housekeeper was already starting to prepare lunch.

Pearl and I decided to split up so that we wouldn't

miss anything. She mewed at Tim, demanding to be picked up, and accompanied him on his way to the library, where he had arranged to meet Ivo. Tim was carrying his laptop with him, so the research would probably take place mainly on the Internet, not in the books kept in the library.

I, on the other hand, trotted along behind Victoria, hoping that I would be allowed to enter the kitchen and not have to eavesdrop outside the door. That was by no means a matter of course—in some households, the kitchen is strictly off-limits to four-leggeds. Sometimes the bedrooms, too. Here in this house, for example, I had noticed that Bastet was not allowed to enter Antonia's bedroom, nor the one that Tobias had been using.

Luisa, however, seemed to be an animal lover, which was fortunate. She let me come into the kitchen with Victoria without much ado. She even tried to be friendly and patted my head. Which made me yelp in pain.

Victoria quickly explained that I had been wounded yesterday during the—second—theft of the Bastet statue, and that I had sustained a thick bump on my head.

"Athos was guarding the statue and I'm sure he defended it valiantly," Victoria said. "Julius must have kicked or punched him. That bastard!"

I was compensated by Luisa with a piece of pie for the injury I'd suffered in the fight, and then I settled down on the pleasantly cool floor and shifted myself to listening.

Apparently Victoria was not nearly as convinced as Tim that Julius Feldmann really was Tobias's murderer. Instead of talking about the escaped art dealer, she first asked Luisa about Leo.

I remembered that Victoria had already suspected the senior citizen influencer—with his delusions of youthfulness—right at the beginning, because he had been hanging around in the suicide forum on the Internet.

However, I wasn't inclined to consider him our main suspect, because for me Feldmann was clearly guilty. After all, the scoundrel had almost murdered me, so he was definitely a violent criminal. He could actually easily have faked his alibi for Tobias's murder, somehow.

Luisa turned out to be an extremely talkative source. She seemed, as Victoria had already suspected, to be very fond of gossip.

"Leo?" she repeated. "Why are you so interested in him? You don't mean to say that he had something to do with the death of my boss? Surely you don't believe that Mr. Unruh was *murdered*? That policewoman, she thinks so too, doesn't she? That's why she keeps coming back..."

The woman's torrent of words spilled over my head, so that my ears started to hurt.

Victoria, too, was having her share of trouble in

steering the conversation in the desired direction. "I think Leo is ... um, acting a little strange," she said vaguely, then prompted Luisa with an encouraging look.

"Strange? Yes, he is. I guess you have to admit that. This business of youthfulness at all costs and constantly putting himself in the limelight on the Internet ... that's really not sane, is it?"

She glanced at the door—which was closed and which made a rather robust impression. The danger of being overheard was probably low in this kitchen, as long as a possible spy didn't have the ears of a dog.

Nevertheless, Luisa now lowered her voice. "They had an argument the other day, you know," she whispered, "my boss and his father."

"Oh yeah?" Victoria acted as if she weren't particularly interested. In truth, she was probably dying to know anything that could possibly be connected with Tobias's death.

Pretty good actress, went through my buzzing head. Not nearly at Pearl's level, but still impressive. The pipsqueak was unsurpassed, especially in the role of the poor little kitten on the verge of starvation.

"Do you know what my boss said?"—Luisa's eyes widened—with pleasure, it seemed to me. She clearly loved being questioned as an important witness. "He said, or rather, he yelled at Leo: *If you don't come to your senses, I'll throw you out! I swear to you. I'm certainly not going to stand idly by while you—*"

"While you ... *what*?" asked Victoria, as if shot out of a gun, with undisguised curiosity in her eyes.

Not such a good actress after all.

Luisa screwed up her face. "Unfortunately, that's all I picked up. At that very moment, Leo's cell phone rang and he stormed out of the room. I just managed to—well, to get out of his way. I didn't mean to eavesdrop, you know. But I'm worried too, aren't I? About both of them, father and son. After all, I've worked here forever. They're almost like family to me."

"I wonder what that exchange of words was about," Victoria mused. "You have no idea at all?" Again she looked at Luisa expectantly, but this time it didn't help at all.

"No, I'm sorry. Although I really racked my brains, of course. But now that the boss is dead, his words sound somehow ... I don't know. Threatening, don't you think? Or am I just being paranoid?"

She didn't give Victoria time to answer. Before my human could even open her mouth, Luisa seemed to come up with a new idea: "Actually, I can't really im-agine Leo being capable of a bloody deed," she said. "Can you, maybe?"

Again there was no time for an answer. She contin-ued immediately—when did she actually breathe? "What about Giorgio, that muscle-headed guy? Fit-ness trainer, doesn't that say it all? Now, *he* looks like a crook to me. Unscrupulous, only concerned for his own advantage. And d'you know what, he also had a fight with the boss, just a few days ago. It got really heated—Mr. Unruh was on the rampage!"

"And what was their argument about?" Victoria managed to ask.

"About the girl, Seschat. Unfortunately the door was closed, so I could only understand half of what was being said. But it seems that this Giorgio guy, well, you know ... that he seduced the poor girl. Or had tried to seduce her? Something like that."

13

When Victoria had said goodbye to the housekeeper, my poor human looked as if she was the one with a buzzing head. My own headache hadn't exactly gotten any better either, but of course, as a detective you cannot let that slow you down.

"Where to now?" I panted at Victoria after we'd left the kitchen. "To Leo's? Should we grill him for a bit, do you think?"

Incredibly, Victoria seemed to understand me this time—or at least she'd just had the same idea I did.

Less than five minutes later, we were sitting across from the senior influencer in his rooms on the first floor. A ring-shaped light was glowing on his desk, in the middle of which he had clamped his cell phone. Apparently he was busy shooting for his Internet fans again, this time without the catfluencer.

He didn't seem too pleased at the two of us visiting him, but was probably too polite to throw us out right away.

"What's up?" he asked curtly.

Victoria was suddenly embarrassed. She certainly didn't want to be rude and ask him straightforwardly about the argument with his son, so she started to stutter.

But then she pulled herself together. "I—um, heard

that your son was supposed to have lost his temper with you. Just the other day, just before he..."

Leo's eyebrows arched upwards. "*You heard*? You don't say. Let me guess: our house dragon has been eavesdropping again, and then she couldn't keep her loose trap shut."

His jaw muscles stood out hard, and he suddenly gave off a very threatening smell. A low growl escaped me, without my having intended it.

Leo looked down at me, but made no comment. Instead, he clicked his tongue. "Terrible woman, that Luisa—I don't know where my son found her. Always eavesdropping, never working. A silly chick in desperate need of a man, if you ask me. I've already tried to set her up with Giorgio, but...."

His eyes narrowed. "She certainly wouldn't be averse, I'd say, but he ... oh, I don't know, maybe he's gay or something. It's all the rage these days, isn't it—being a homosexual? If I were younger and still interested in love...."

He let his gaze wander into nowhere for a moment.

When he'd regained his composure, he looked at Victoria and said, "I really don't owe you an account, but yes, my son and I had an argument. That happened occasionally. So what?"

"What was it about, if you don't mind me asking? He threatened to throw you out of the house? Why is that?"

"That's really none of your damn business," Leo

hurled at her, seized with sudden anger.

I came to my paws. Would I have to intervene here soon? If Victoria kept provoking the old man like this, she was risking her neck. And this senior biped was anything but a weakling. He could easily have strangled her with his bare hands.

Of course it would not come to that. After all I was present to protect my human. This time I refrained from growling though, in order not to heat up the atmosphere between the two humans even further.

The next moment, Leo suddenly laughed. "Oh, what the heck—do you think I would have been bothered if my son really had thrown me out? He would have been able to; after all, it's his house. *Was* his house," he corrected himself. "But that wouldn't have made me homeless. I make a high six figure income as an influencer, in case you were wondering. So I could always have rented a fancy place of my own if I'd wanted to."

He ran his fingers over his chin and leaned forward a bit.

"You're not going to get anywhere with this," he said in such an ominous tone that it made the hairs on the back of my neck stand up. "You can play private detective all you want; I already told you what we're dealing with here. With a curse—which is on that hideous cat statue. Now you'd better get out of here, I'm busy."

Victoria stood up, but let her gaze rest on Leo for a

few moments. What was going on in her head? Did she really suspect him of murder? Did she just not dare to tell it to his face, because she feared for her life?

I stood next to her, lifted my head and gave one short sharp yelp. "You really don't have to be afraid," I encouraged her. "I'll take care of you."

She patted my head, lost in thought. Pain flashed through me and I quickly ducked away under her hand.

"Oh, sorry!" she gasped. "I forgot all about your bump...."

Her voice died away. And finally she took her eyes off Leo, mumbled a few indistinct words of farewell and turned to leave. She didn't let me know what was going on in her mind, even when it was just the two of us.

Next I accompanied Victoria to the library, to check on Tim's progress with his research.

Pearl, who had clearly just been napping on the fluffy carpet, jumped up and ran toward me as we entered the library.

"No progress here," she reported to me. "They're still as knowledgeable about the statue as they were some hours ago."

I looked over at Tim and Ivo, who were sitting next to each other at the large table where Melissa had conducted her interrogations earlier. Both men were staring down at their quietly whirring laptops.

Tim rose now and walked toward Victoria with a pained expression in his eyes.

"Nothing useful so far, I'm afraid," he said, confirming Pearl's words—just as I was about to reproach her for sleeping on duty again.

Ivo stood up as well.

"There's something strange about this statue," he commented. "I remember that Tobias remained vague about the provenance of this magnificent piece; it supposedly came from the tomb of a pharaoh's daughter, but he didn't know any details about that. Or was it that he just didn't want to share them? And Julius told us some stories about the former owners, always hinting at this supposed curse of Bastet. However, he did not mention any specific names—quite the discreet art dealer." He sighed, looking very tired.

"And there's nothing on the Internet or social media about it?" asked Victoria. "Hasn't this thing ever been sold at an auction? Or displayed in an exhibition, or maybe featured in a newspaper article somewhere?"

Tim and Ivo shrugged their shoulders almost simultaneously. "Doesn't look like it," Ivo said.

"We'll keep at it," Tim averred. "I'm not going to give up that easily."

But that's exactly what he did, albeit a few hours later.

I'd stayed with Pearl while Victoria left the men to themselves again. The afternoon passed with more Internet research, followed by frustration and perplexity.

At some point, Ivo threw in the towel. "I'm sorry, but I've had enough for today," he said in apology. "I need to get some fresh air."

"Good idea," Tim replied immediately. He didn't seem particularly eager to stare at his laptop screen any longer either, as they had spent an entire day without any useful result.

"Shall we perhaps take a short stroll through the valley?" he suggested to Ivo. "The path is fantastically beautiful."

"Yeah, sure. Why not?"

The two of them headed towards the door. I felt like joining them, but Pearl finally wanted to take a nap. She had dutifully kept watch by my side all afternoon, listening with me to the murmurs and sounds of frustration from the two men—probably to prove to me what an eager detective she was. In between, I had described Victoria's conversations with Luisa and Leo to her, and she had listened to me most attentively.

So I decided she should enjoy her siesta while I would accompany the two men on their walk in the woods.

"I'll see you later then, okay?" I said to her.

She again emitted that very un-catlike grunt I've described before, and curled up for her nap. Tim and Ivo, on the other hand, were already leaving the library. I ran after them.

Then, however, Tim stopped abruptly and squatted down. "Hold on, Ivo, wait. You've got something on your pants there."

He plucked something tiny from the dark woolen fabric, but did not carelessly toss it aside. He looked at it briefly but intently, then let it disappear into the back pocket of his jeans.

"Just a crumb," he explained to Ivo, who was looking at him in amazement. "Now you're free of it. Shall we go?"

Ivo nodded and started moving again.

I had seen clearly though that the tiny thing Tim had picked off Ivo's trouser leg was not a crumb—but rather a few of the tiny but aggressively hairy fibers of a burdock plant.

14

As soon as I'd gotten back from my walk with the two men, I went to see Pearl. She was actually still asleep, the little lazybones.

Perhaps in my excitement I woke her up a little too brusquely, stammering incoherent nonsense. "A burr! On Ivo's trouser leg. Must have been the same pants he was wearing the night Tobias died. I noticed a burr then, too. They're so persistent, the little buggers. A few always stick somewhere, and at the bottom of a pair of dark wool pants ... with the bad eyes of the bipeds—do you understand? Ivo certainly must have overlooked it. But it proves that he was near the thistle thicket. Where we found the statue later. He must have stolen it from the house the night it disappeared and Tobias died, and disposed of it there!"

"Take a breath, Athos!" Pearl replied, instead of praising me for my investigative tour de force. Then she actually went and asked me to explain everything to her all over again.

So I repeated what I'd said, perhaps expressing myself a little more clearly this time. Anyway, I managed to make Pearl understand that Ivo had to be guilty. Of theft in any case—but maybe murder, too?

"Why did he steal the statue and then throw it into that burr thicket?" Pearl wanted to know. "If not to distract from the murder? But Julius—he wanted to get his hands on it too? What on earth is it about that statue that makes the two-leggeds so crazy?"

After dinner, Victoria decided to have a conversation—woman to woman, so to speak—with Seschat. Tim was not to be present, in the hope that the girl would be more open to a private tête-à-tête.

Pearl and I were allowed to participate, of course; we were more conducive to a relaxed conversational atmosphere, rather than a hindrance, Victoria had decided. She was right, of course.

Talking to Seschat was clearly easier for her than questioning Leo Unruh had been before. And the opportunity arose almost effortlessly.

Today dinner was served on the terrace again, and Seschat remained at the table after the meal. Lost in thought; depressed.

Victoria approached her, told her in her gentle therapist's tone of voice that she would like to talk to her about something, and invited her to go for a *little walk with Athos and Pearl.*

Who could resist?

This time we didn't hike through the Helenental, but stayed in the villa's private park, which was spacious enough to wander around in for a while. Pearl and I kept ourselves inconspicuously in the background, pretending to be interested in the fauna and flora on our meandering route, but of course pricking up our ears so that we didn't miss a word of the conversation.

Victoria automatically took on the role of the empathic psychologist and comforted the poor girl. Seschat really was not in a good state. She was pale, had hardly eaten anything at dinner and had spoken very little.

"I have a bit of a tricky question for you," Victoria began, after first making some reassuring small talk. "It might be connected to the death of your father—or it might not," she added quickly, "but I think it's important that we get clarity on what really happened to him."

"Clarity?" Seschat asked in alarm. "He fell down the stairs ... didn't he?"

Victoria skirted the question. "I'd like to talk to you about Giorgio. Has he—bothered you in any way, Seschat?" That was quite abrupt. And our human did seem a little nervous.

"What? What gave you that idea?" Seschat stopped abruptly and performed a half turn, as if she wanted to retreat right away.

"Sorry," Victoria said quickly. She touched Seschat gently on the shoulder. "Shall we walk a little further?" She started moving again, slowly but determinedly—and Seschat finally followed her, though with little enthusiasm.

"All I care about is understanding why your father

had to die," Victoria continued. "He had a fight with Giorgio because of you. You know that, don't you?" She looked inquiringly at the girl.

Seschat turned her head away.

"You want your father's death to be resolved, too, I imagine," insisted Victoria. "And you know some-thing you haven't told the police yet. Am I not right?"

Again Seschat stopped, this time so abruptly that I almost ran into her.

Which at least blocked her way back toward the house.

"You're giving me the creeps," she told Victoria. "It feels like you're looking right into my head."

"I'm really just trying to help," said Victoria, but I perceived that she was also uncomfortable. The smell she gave off on such occasions was unmistakable; she was sweating and feeling cold at the same time. I can't express it any better.

"She wants to be a sleuth, but is still ashamed of her pervasive curiosity," Pearl, self-proclaimed expert on humans, put my perceptions into words. "She's going to have to get over that. As an investigator, you can't always be cuddly."

"You of all people shouldn't say that, who's always beguiling the bipeds with your *cute-kitten* act."

"It's not my fault I'm irresistible," Pearl replied in a flirtatious tone.

Victoria had probably also concluded that she needed to be persistent, even if she didn't want to offend Seschat.

"You can trust me," she promised the youngster. "I won't tell the police anything you confide in me—on my word of honor. But we need to help clear up your father's death, and find out how the theft of this statue is connected." She tilted her head. "Do you happen to know anything about that, maybe, Seschat?"

The girl stepped from one foot to the other and suddenly smelled even more nervous than Victoria did.

"Promise you won't tell anyone? Your word of honor? Because I don't want Father's reputation ... to be ruined, even if he's dead now, you understand?"

"Of course," Victoria said quickly. "No one wants that, I assure you."

Seschat narrowed her eyes. "Is it true that your friend Tim—that he was doing research with Ivo all day? On the Bastet statue. Luisa mentioned it..."

Luisa. She was really the top source of information in the house.

"That's right," Victoria said. "We'd like to understand what's so valuable about this statue that Julius Feldmann stole it, brutalizing my dog in the process, after having sold it to your father himself not so long ago."

"Do you think Julius murdered my father?" Seschat's voice broke, becoming almost as shrill as a bat's whistle.

"It's possible," Victoria said cautiously. "Do you

know why this statue is so—sought after? Does it have some special value that we don't know about?"

"It's not about its value," Seschat began. "I mean, it *was* expensive. Father had to shell out quite a bit for it, as far as I know...."

"But?" probed Victoria.

The smells that the two women were emitting really were a violent mix. Fear, worry, frustration ... I only ever get myself worked up into such a state when I have to go to the vet. Especially for dental care; that's what I hate the most.

"The statue—it was illegal," Seschat suddenly blurted out. "I think that's why Julius wanted it back so badly: so that the police wouldn't find out about his business."

"*Illegal*?" Victoria repeated with a confused look on her face. "What do you mean by that? Not stolen, was it?"

Seschat grimaced. "I don't know exactly, either. I just overheard a conversation—when Dad bought the statue from Julius. It must have been smuggled out of Egypt, and found there during an illegal excavation. From what I understand there are official, authorized excavations ... but the pieces found in the process usually have to stay in Egypt, or they are loaned to museums. And then I guess there's such a thing as modern tomb raiders, or that's what my father called them. They secretly search for ancient graves, dig up the treasures themselves and then sell them under the table to collectors. Through dealers like Julius."

"And your father knew that the statue had left Egypt this way? And all the stories Julius told about its previous owners were just made up?"

Seschat nodded hesitantly. "My father had probably never acquired a black-market piece like this before. And I think Julius deals in legal stuff most of the time, too—but apparently the temptation was especially strong with this statue. Because it was rare, or of special artistic value? Well preserved? I have no idea. Anyway, Dad was willing to buy the statue even though he knew its provenance was ... well, unlawful."

Pearl raised her head and looked at me. "So now we know what really went on between Tobias and Seschat. She was blackmailing her father because she knew about his illegal purchase! When she argued with him about Giorgio, she threatened him: *I'll take you out!* She didn't mean she was going to kill him."

"But only that she would report his black-market purchase of the statue to the authorities?" I continued the thought.

"Exactly. That's why she could do whatever she wanted; Tobias was at her mercy, and so she was suddenly spending a lot more money than before. And he couldn't just forbid her to date Giorgio, either. He had to try to bribe him in order to get him to stay away from his daughter."

I remembered Leo Unruh's words: that Tobias had

let his daughter get away with far too much lately, since the statue had been in the house. The spry senior had blamed it on the curse he so stubbornly believed in, but the answer was much simpler, much more down to earth. Ever since Tobias had acquired the statue, and Seschat happened to have witnessed his conversation with Julius Feldmann, his own daughter had been blackmailing him.

Victoria knew nothing about it, of course. But did she perhaps suspect it?

"Why didn't you say a word about this before?" she asked Seschat now. "It's very important information, don't you think?"

"Because she had a guilty conscience, of course!" meowed Pearl. "She didn't want to be exposed as a blackmailer."

"I didn't want Dad's reputation ruined!" said Seschat. "I told you that already." She stared at her feet, avoiding Victoria's gaze. "Do you think Julius killed my father—because of that statue? So his fishy business practices wouldn't be exposed?"

"It's possible," said Victoria. "In any case, the police must learn that the cat goddess is looted art. That Julius not only had a motive to make the statue disappear, but possibly also to take your father's life. Maybe Tobias came to the conclusion that he should report the illegal transaction, even if he himself was involved in it, and Julius wanted to prevent that at all costs. Something like that is conceivable."

"But you promised to keep this a secret!" Seschat complained.

"Don't worry," Victoria replied. "We'll keep your father out of this completely. We can tell Ms. Funke that Tim's research into the statue has led him to suspect that it has been brought into the country illegally. Your father could have bought it in good faith from Julius Feldmann. No one can now prove that he knew anything about the illegal origin of the statue ... as long as you say nothing."

"I certainly won't!"

"Then your father's reputation won't be damaged. But the police will know that Julius had a motive to steal the statue ... and perhaps to do worse. And that can be very important to the investigation."

Seschat stood there, undecided. She wanted her father's death to be solved, I was sure of that—but she also wanted to avoid her own little blackmail plot coming to light. And perhaps she really did care about her father's reputation.

"Shall we go back to the house and talk to Tim?" Victoria suggested.

"Alright," said Seschat, and the two humans slowly started moving away.

15

"We need to find out if Julius Feldmann really does have an alibi for Tobias's murder," Tim told Victoria after listening to Seschat's story.

The little blackmailer had gone to her room after my humans had once again assured her that they would present only Feldmann as the guilty party to the police, in the matter of the illegal origin of the statue. Tobias could no longer be held accountable for the purchase of looted art anyway—after all, he was no longer alive to answer charges.

"If we call Ms. Funke now, we should try to ask her about Julius's alibi as well," Victoria said. "Hopefully she will be able to tell us whether or not it has already been confirmed."

"I'll see what I can get out of her," Tim said. "I'm afraid the chief inspector isn't very talkative."

He, too, exuded a scent cocktail of excitement, nervousness and fear as he immediately reached for his cell phone and called the policewoman.

But his voice did not betray him; it sounded firm and calm. In clear tones, he informed Ms. Funke that his research on the statue had led him to a promising lead. He expressed the suspicion that Bastet had possibly come from an illegal excavation and into the possession of Julius Feldmann via the black market.

Victoria, Pearl and I were able to follow the conversation because Tim had put his cell phone on speaker.

"And that's probably why Julius stole the statue after we found it in the garden," he concluded his report. "So that it wouldn't fall into your hands, and so your experts wouldn't find out that the piece was looted art."

Melissa thanked him and tried to end the conversation right afterwards.

"Just a moment, please!" Tim said quickly. "Have you been able to track down Mr. Feldmann in the meantime?" he asked.

The chief inspector hesitated. I could hear her breathing through the phone, but she said nothing. She was probably debating with herself how much she was allowed to reveal about her investigation.

Tim seemed to have suspected the same thing. "Look, Ms. Funke—we're really trying to help, you can see that, can't you? We tracked down the statue for you and put you on Mr. Feldmann's trail after it was stolen again. Well, strictly speaking our dog found it, but that's still a point in our favor, I think. And I've just given you a possible motive for why this man might have murdered Mr. Unruh..."

"We have indeed been able to track down Mr. Feldmann," Melissa said, cutting him off. She sounded frustrated. "We will now, of course, question him about the new leads you have just given us. We're doing a thorough job, I can assure you."

"I certainly don't doubt that," Tim said in a conciliatory tone.

She gave a low growl. "It's just that we can't prove Mr. Feldmann stole the statue—or indeed any involvement he may have had in Tobias Unruh's death. We couldn't find any footprints of his in the garden where your dog was guarding the statue and it was stolen. The ground was dry and on the gravel path it would have been even harder to...."

She broke off. "In any case, Mr. Feldmann testified that he merely left the villa last night to get his mind off things, that he drove his car to Vienna to go to a bar, and we have been able to verify his claim. Also, he allowed us to search his Vienna apartment."

"Where you didn't find the statue," Tim said.

"Indeed we did not. He also claims that he hadn't been in the garden at all last night, apart from going to dinner, and he denies any knowledge that you had recovered the statue. Or rather, that your dog had."

"But he could have quickly hidden Bastet somewhere on the way to this bar," Tim objected. "In a locker or somewhere, I don't know. There are hundreds of possibilities. It's not like the thing is really big or bulky."

"Of course. It's just that we can't prove anything like that—not yet. Not even the original theft on the night Mr. Unruh died. However, I will now call in my relevant colleagues and pursue the new lead you have given me, the one about the looted art. Maybe we'll get somewhere that way."

"And the forensics?" Tim asked quickly, before Melissa could finally hang up. "Any info yet on how Tobias really died? Maybe someone had a hand in his accident after all."

"We'll have the results by tomorrow morning," Melissa said. "And now good evening, Mr. Mortensen. And thank you again for your help."

She disconnected the call before Tim could say anything further. He'd also had no opportunity to ask Ms. Funke about Feldmann's alibi, as he'd intended to do. But perhaps he would not have received an answer in any case.

Our two-leggeds soon went to bed, both lost in thought and at a loss for words.

What about Ivo Lindquist, I asked myself. Why had that burdock seed been stuck to his trouser leg?

16

I wasn't able to pursue that thought any further, though, because that very night the murderer of Tobias Unruh revealed himself to us. And when I say that the confession came most unexpectedly for Pearl and me, I am probably understating it.

I must also confess that we owed this circumstance, this quasi-gifted solution to our criminal case, more or less to a coincidence and not to our ingenious sleuthing. But a good detective must set his vanity aside when it comes to solving a murder. And Tobias Unruh had indeed been murdered; we now knew that for a certainty.

After our two-leggeds had gone to bed early, Pearl and I decided to trudge down to the kitchen. On the one hand we needed something to drink, but on the other we were hoping that Luisa might still be working late, and that some treat would be up for grabs.

However, as we were about to run down to the lower floor, we noticed Bastet the house cat below us on the stairs. She had almost reached the ground floor, but she was either careless, lost in thought, or otherwise engaged, because she did not notice our presence right away. And it was only for this reason that we could make a decisive observation: she was limping—on the right front paw. And it was quite obvious to even the most casual observer.

I didn't at first attach any particular importance to it, I must confess. But Pearl stopped abruptly, and her whiskers began to vibrate ... a sure sign that something didn't suit my royal tigress, four-pawed diva and recently-initiated catfluencer.

"What's wrong?" I hissed at her. Probably too loudly, because at the bottom of the stairs Bastet whirled around, startled. She stared at us for a moment out of her deep green eyes, but then calmly continued on her way. Apparently she was also headed for the kitchen.

"Look, Athos, now suddenly she's not limping anymore," whispered Pearl, so softly that only I could hear her. It was little more than a thought she sent toward me.

"Yeah ... so?" I answered, still dumbfounded.

"On the afternoon of the day Tobias died, I saw her prancing around in a tree outside in the park—in full possession of her grace and agility. Not a trace of an injury."

I refrained from another *yeah, so?* but just let Pearl continue talking.

"Today at dinner, when she stopped by the table to grab a few pieces of chicken, she didn't limp at all either."

I sat down on my hind paws, which was not really comfortable on the steps. Would Pearl actually get to the point now?

Instead of finally enlightening me, she went on to a contemplate the taste of chicken, and compared it to salmon, her personal favorite. "Chicken is kind of mundane, don't you think, Athos? It tastes so..."

She seemed to be searching for the right word.

"Like chicken?" I offered.

She wrinkled her nose. "Very funny."

"What's this about Bastet, now?" I asked impatiently. "She must have hurt herself after dinner—or what are you getting at?"

"Don't you understand? Where and how is she supposed to have hurt herself? After dinner she went into the house—where we met her again once or twice. And on those occasions, she was clearly moving around completely normally. Just like at dinner, too."

I understood less and less. "You mean to say she was just pretending when she went down the stairs? That she was only faking the limp? But what on earth for? She didn't even notice we were behind her. I'm sure she thought she was all alone."

Pearl suddenly came so close in front of me that I could only see her blue eyes in my vision. Even in the semi-darkness of the entrance hall, they shone like two sparkling gems.

"That's exactly my point," she murmured to me excitedly. "She thought she was alone, unobserved. She wasn't pretending, Athos. She let herself go! She must have hurt herself, sometime since I saw her up in that tree a few days ago. Because on that occasion, I'm sure her four paws were still intact. For all her self-control and suppression of the pain, she could never have been prancing around on the branches like that if she had been injured then."

"She could have only just hurt herself," I said, "right before we saw her walk down the stairs."

"And where, pray tell, would a cat hurt her leg here in the house? I already talked about that, Athos. Are you listening to me?"

I began to suspect what she was getting at.

"She had an ... altercation, you're trying to say, and hurt herself in the process? A fight or something that took place sometime after that climbing session in the garden that you witnessed, and that she's trying to hide from us and from the two-leggeds?"

"You're finally getting it," Pearl assented. "We need to have a serious word with her. She owes us an explanation! The fact that she's trying to hide the injury is highly suspicious."

She didn't wait to hear what I had to say, but moved down the last few steps, hopping like a little rabbit, and then ran at a sprinting pace toward the kitchen.

We found Bastet in front of the water bowl; there was nothing to be seen of Luisa. It was dark in the kitchen, except for some moonlight falling through the windows.

"How did you come to be hurt, Bastet?" Pearl came to the point immediately and without showing all that much empathy.

The cat stopped her slobbering and raised her head. She looked at Pearl with a bored expression, while she didn't even acknowledge me.

"Were you attacked?" Pearl continued, unperturbed. "Like Athos? Like your human? Why did you hide this from us?"

She strode courageously—or should I say she was tired of living?—towards her clearly larger conspecific, until the noses of the two had almost collided.

I followed her hurriedly. Once again she had overestimated herself, provoking an animal that could quickly become dangerous to her. She'd asked Bastet only a few questions, but her tone came across as accusatory, as if we were in a two-legged courtroom.

Bastet looked down upon the tiny one in silence, but didn't retreat an inch. I registered how her back had begun to arch and that Pearl's neck hairs had stood up at the same time.

I did not wait until the two hotheads had extended their claws, and blood had been spilled, but went resolutely between them.

I gave Pearl a gentle nose bump, which pushed her a bit away from Bastet, and then placed myself in front of the house cat.

Bastet's eyes narrowed—but then she suddenly sat down nonchalantly on her hind paws and wrapped her tail around her body.

"You superb detectives," she grumbled condescendingly. "You think you're so smart, don't you, huh? You could snoop around here for a few more weeks and still never stumble upon the truth. How pathetic."

"Then enlighten us if you're so much smarter," I snapped back.

Bastet's whiskers twitched—as I had often observed with Pearl, only it didn't seem the least bit droll on this overbearing cat.

"I don't want to be petty," she said, "so I'll give you a leg up. Maybe this way I'll finally get rid of you. This house is *my turf,* and you two ... you're just annoying me."

She rose from her hind paws and defiantly thrust out her gray-spotted head.

"It was *I* who killed my human," she announced, sounding unabashedly proud. "I ran between his legs at the top of the stairs. With that I brought him down, so that he fell to his death. And *in the process* I hurt myself, you wise guys. Nobody attacked me—I just was kicked when Tobias tripped over me. So now you know."

With that, she turned away and once again busied herself with the drinking bowl. As if she had to wet her throat after her dramatic words.

To be honest, I was speechless. I really hadn't expected that.

Pearl looked equally befuddled, but regained her composure more quickly. "Why did you murder him? Did you hate your human so much, then?" she asked

Bastet, who had turned her back to us, sipping her water with emphatic pleasure.

As if in slow motion, the house cat finally turned around again. However, she ignored us, walking royally towards the door.

But the words she dropped in passing we heard clearly: "I loved him, before I learned what a monster he was."

Need I mention that Pearl and I spent the night in a state of utmost confusion?

Of course, we first tried to follow Bastet and to elicit further details from her, but that was futile. She didn't dignify us with so much as a glance or a word, no matter how we bombarded her with questions. Finally, she slipped out through one of the automatic cat doors and into the nocturnal park, no longer hiding her limp from us. On the contrary, she moved as proudly as a warrior, displaying her battle wounds as a badge of honor.

I stopped Pearl from following her. I couldn't fit through the cat door myself, and I certainly couldn't let the pipsqueak run after a mad creature who had just outed herself as a murderer.

Instead we retreated to the kitchen for a war council: I lay down on the cool tiles, and Pearl dropped onto my paw, perplexed.

"Do you think she's telling the truth?" she asked.

"What reason would she have to confess to a murder she didn't commit?"

"But why, Athos? Why did she kill her human? What did she mean by saying he was a monster?"

I didn't know the answer to these questions, and I had no reply to Pearl's next one either. "How are we going to explain this to the police? That we caught Tobias's killer?"

"More like that she revealed herself to us," I objected.

"You mean ... extenuating circumstances?"

"I mean—forget it, Pearl! Surely the police have no jurisdiction over murderous cats?"

Pearl meowed miserably. "You're right about that, I'm afraid. But then what are we supposed to do? Just let her get away with her insane act?"

"Could her comment that Tobias was a monster have been referring to the fact that he acquired the Bastet statue illegally?" I mused, because Pearl's questions truly were unanswerable. "That it was stolen goods from a tomb?"

"That may go against the laws of the two-leggeds," Pearl said. "But to us—and to Bastet, I think—it makes no difference who is looting their graves. Whether it's bipeds with some official permission, or whether they're doing it secretly."

"Hmm, I suppose," I grumbled. It probably was a dead end. An oppressive silence, born of perplexity, settled over us.

At some point I heard Pearl's soft snoring next to me, and shortly thereafter I must have fallen asleep as well. But I continued to dream for a long time about killer cats, murderous goddesses, and bronze statues that came to life as though in a horror movie.

17

The next morning the police returned with news that surprised everyone, especially the two of us, since we had heard the confession of Tobias Unruh's murderer only last night.

When Melissa Funke came into the house, stomped into the breakfast room, and informed the two-leggeds of the results of the autopsy, Pearl and I had just been thinking hard about how to pass on our knowledge of the four-pawed murderess to our humans.

"Tobias Unruh was not dead after he fell down the stairs," Melissa announced—her gaze wandering intently over the faces of the bipeds. She was probably hoping to be able to tell from their expressions who was taking this news with genuine amazement, and who was merely pretending to be surprised—because they had long since known exactly how Tobias had actually died.

"The fall merely stunned him," she specified, "and he broke some bones. But the death in fact occurred by suffocation, and someone must have had a hand in it. So this is therefore now a murder investigation. I must ask you all to remain at our disposal for further questioning."

With that she left the room again, but Tim and Victoria jumped up and followed her. Pearl and I did the same, of course—after all, we didn't want to miss a word.

In the entrance hall, our two-leggeds and the two police detectives came to a stop.

"Do you have any more information for me, Mr. Mortensen? Dr. Adler?" the chief inspector asked in an emphatically neutral tone.

"We—no, not really," said Tim, "We just wanted to know if..."

"Have you been able to confirm Julius Feldmann's alibi in the meantime?" Victoria came to his rescue. She looked just as surprised as he did, but had apparently gotten herself under control a little more. "Was he really on that video call with a client the night of the murder? At the time Tobias fell down the stairs?"

"I really can't discuss the details of this case with you, especially since it now involves murder," Melissa said. "I'm sure you can understand that."

She was about to start moving away again, but now Tim took the floor from Victoria. This time he sounded much more determined, and more self-confident.

"We can be of use to you in the investigation," he said. "We've already proven that, haven't we? Here in the villa, we have an insider's perspective, so to speak. People will talk to us rather than to you, informally, without fear of saying the wrong thing. Don't you think? And we gave you a decisive hint regarding Mr. Feldmann and the statue, namely that it has to be looted art. Have you been able to confirm that in the meantime?"

Melissa inhaled audibly, then exhaled. She stood there indecisively for a moment, then said, "My colleagues are on the case. And if you really want to know—yes, we have been able to confirm his alibi. Mr. Feldmann can therefore be ruled out as the murderer."

"But that also means he couldn't have stolen the Bastet statue," Tim concluded. "The first time, I mean. Because it must have been taken either just before or right after the time Tobias was murdered."

Melissa indicated a nod.

Tim was increasingly getting into the swing of things. He spoke faster now, and could hardly hide his excitement. To me he smelled as if he were on a wild chase, with the prey right in front of his eyes.

"That means whoever choked Tobias at the foot of the stairs grabbed the statue, hid it outside in the garden, and then smashed the glass door to fake a break-in," he said. "Probably because he knew that Tobias's death would not pass as a mere accident. He had to expect that death by asphyxiation could be proved."

"You really know your stuff," Melissa said. She was looking at him with a slightly unfriendly expression, but she didn't smell angry.

"Look," she went on, "I can't stop you from snooping around the house on your own, and I will admit that this case does have its challenges. We don't have any usable evidence on the body that would point to a specific suspect, and so far there are no witness statements that get us anywhere. Everybody claims to have been in their room and to have seen nothing and heard nothing. In that respect, I will certainly not refuse if you can provide us with some clues. But I have to bring two things to your attention. First, if you obstruct our investigation, that's a criminal offense—and I'm not going to treat it as a peccadillo."

"Sure," Victoria muttered.

"And second, for heaven's sake, be careful! You must never underestimate a murderer. He is here among you, that much is certain—and he will certainly not hesitate to strike a second time if someone shows themselves to be a threat to him. Do you understand that?"

"Perfectly," Tim said. "We certainly won't be reckless."

"We already have some experience with killers, you know," Victoria said.

"Excuse me?" Melissa exclaimed. "What's that supposed to mean?"

Victoria suddenly looked a little embarrassed. "Well, we've been involved in solving murders a whole three times now. Since I inherited my father's dog—and a friend's kitten."

"Then I guess it's your pets that are cursed," the policewoman joked in a bitter tone, "and not that Bastet statue. Usually, it's quite the rare occurrence for an average citizen to witness a single murder case in his or her lifetime. But three at once? Or even four, now."

Melissa looked down at us as if we ourselves had been guilty of the murders in which we'd been involved, and which we had ultimately solved.

Turning again to Victoria and Tim, she repeated, "As I've said, please be careful. Call me anytime, for whatever reason!"

Tim and Victoria promised they would do so, and then Melissa and her assistant took their leave. Of course we would see them again soon; that was absolutely clear to me.

"Cursed? Us?" Pearl complained to me after the police detectives had disappeared. "Is she in her right mind? And Victoria forgot to mention that *we* solved those murder cases!"

"Don't fret," I tried to comfort her. "That's just the way people are."

"Pah!"

Pearl narrowed her eyes into dark slits, then began pacing around in circles, talking excitedly to me. "So what does this mean for our investigation? We thought we had the murderer—Bastet. She herself is firmly of the opinion that she killed Tobias."

"Apparently he wasn't quite dead when he landed at the bottom of the stairs," I said.

"Looks like it. Bastet couldn't have suffocated him, though."

I had to think about how Pearl sometimes snuggled up to my muzzle in her sleep—where she seemed to assume the craziest positions—making me almost drown in cat hair. Not a nice death.

Tobias, however, had not died in this way, of that I was sure. A biped must have helped him toward his final end. Someone who'd heard his fall, found him at the bottom of the stairs and finished him off instead of calling an ambulance.

Apparently Bastet was not the only one who'd hated the master of the house; we didn't know what motive she'd had for her insidious attack, and what had driven the unknown biped—the real murderer—to do his deed was also still in the dark.

"Oh God, I'm such an ass!" Tim, who was standing right behind me, cried out suddenly. I leaped forward in surprise. Then I whirled around.

"Sorry, my boy," he gasped. "I just remembered something!"

With glittering eyes, he turned to Victoria. "The burrs!" he shouted ... then he ran toward the exit and disappeared into the garden.

Victoria remained behind, puzzled. Pearl and I, on the other hand, raced after him. We just made it through the door that led to the outside before it slammed shut and crushed us.

In the park, Tim hurried toward the thicket where we had been able to track down the Bastet statue thanks to our witness, the bat.

He went down on his knees on the gravel path, pretty much in the exact spot where I had put the statue after I'd found it, and near where the closest burdock thistle bushes were already looking for victims.

Then he reached into the back pocket of his jeans and pulled out the dried burdock remnants he had picked off of Ivo's pants yesterday.

To my shame, I have to admit that I had completely forgotten this important clue—in view of all the events that had unfolded so dramatically the previous night and this morning.

Pearl looked even more confused than I did. Had I even told her about Tim's burdock find? I couldn't remember.

Victoria came toward us at a run. Apparently she had followed us after all. When she reached us, she crouched down next to Tim. He was in the process of comparing the thistle remains he had collected with the specimens that grew everywhere here. He might want to be a historian now, but he had not yet lost his gardener's eye.

"They're the same thistles," he told Victoria. "I found them on Ivo's trouser leg yesterday, and I'm pretty sure he was wearing the same pants the night we found Tobias dead. And I haven't seen these plants in any other place here in the garden. They seem to grow only in this thicket—where the Bastet statue must have been hidden before Athos and Pearl recovered it. Do you know what that means?"

"That we should call Ms. Funke?" said Victoria.

18

The chief inspector promised our humans that she would return to the villa as soon as possible. It would take some time, she said, because she had just received a lead regarding the whereabouts of the Bastet statue and was on her way to the address with her colleagues.

Apparently, one of Julius Feldmann's employees had mentioned an old warehouse that had not been used for some time, but which was still in Mr. Feldmann's possession. It was the ideal place to hide a statue that had to be stored away for a few years before Julius could hope to safely sell it to another collector.

In any case, Melissa eagerly absorbed the information about the thistles, and Tim and Victoria now seemed convinced that Ivo had to be the murderer of Tobias Unruh.

After all, Julius Feldmann could not have killed him, as he had an alibi for the night of the murder—which had now been confirmed, according to Melissa. He was probably only guilty of seizing the opportunity the night before last to grab the statue after I had tracked it down in the undergrowth.

Julius was an unscrupulous art dealer and an animal abuser, but apparently not a murderer.

"The thistles are merely circumstantial evidence,

not proof," Pearl said in that know-it-all tone of voice she often displayed when taking on the role of master detective. "What reason could Ivo have had to kill Tobias?"

Of course I didn't know the answer to that. He seemed to have just as little motive for this deed as Bastet, the killer cat, who had brought down her own human on the stairs with murderous intent.

But I remembered something that had struck me at the very beginning of our stay at Villa Unruh.

"Tobias and Ivo, they were supposed to be really close friends," I said to Pearl. "And as far as Tobias was concerned, that's exactly the impression I got. He was always kind and gracious when he was dealing with Ivo. Ivo, on the other hand ... he treated Tobias kind of strangely, I thought. He seemed so—I don't know. Cool? Distant? Even Tim noticed that, remember? He mentioned it to Victoria when we took that walk in the woods, the morning after Tobias died."

"That's right," Pearl agreed. "But what does it mean? Do you think Ivo and Tobias had a fight? Was it so bad that it caused Ivo to want to kill his former friend, when he found him helpless at the bottom of the stairs in the middle of the night?"

"Ivo must definitely have heard Tobias fall, the impact down in the hall," I said. "It's no wonder, since his room is close by. The thing about the earplugs he always uses at night ... I'm sure it was a lie."

"And instead of calling an ambulance, he took the

opportunity to squeeze his friend's mouth and nose shut until he choked to death," Pearl said.

"We should talk to Bastet again," I suggested. "Did she really push Tobias down the stairs—and Ivo just finished him off? Or did she tell us that story to cover for him?"

"Why would she want to cover for him?" protested Pearl. "He's not her human, is he? I'm sure they don't know each other very well. He doesn't come into the house that often, does he?"

Questions and more questions.

"Maybe we have to consider the possibility that Bastet did suffocate Tobias after all," Pearl abruptly suggested a new direction. She didn't seem to have noticed that she was contradicting her earlier assertion.

Master detective, my ass.

"What if Bastet sat on his face?" she pondered with a thoughtful expression. "After all, we like to get comfortable on our humans even in peacetime—on their chests, their heads, their faces—if they will let us. Their breath makes for such a nice, warm steam massage, doesn't it?"

"Look at me, Pearl. Do you think I've ever tried putting myself on a biped's face? Or even just on their chest? They'd stifle, wouldn't they? As big as I am," I added quickly.

Not that Pearl would end up thinking that I considered myself heavy. I was just *big. Strong.* Not built to nap on our wimpy humans.

"Anyway," said the tiny one, "I just want to note that a cat can also suffocate a human if she puts her mind to it, especially if he is already stunned or paralyzed by a fall down the stairs."

"Let's talk to Bastet again," I said. "Before we get ourselves all hot and bothered here."

I honestly did not believe in this new theory. Cat hairs would have been found in Tobias' mouth and throat if Bastet had suffocated him. And that would certainly not have escaped the coroner's attention. Or had it? Maybe because he just didn't expect a cat to be the murderer?

We found Bastet outside in the garden, taking a nap on the low-hanging branch of a beech tree.

At first she looked down on us with ennui, as if on some annoying subjects who had disturbed her pharaonic highness during her beauty sleep. But then she was at least gracious enough to come down to us on the ground.

Pearl took over the conversation, to which I had no objections—from cat to cat, so to speak.

She first reported to Bastet the result of the coroner's medical examination, that Tobias had been suffocated after initially surviving his fall down the stairs.

"You didn't mention anything about that to us,"

Pearl said. "So I take it you didn't choke him?"

Bastet said nothing in reply. If her gray ears hadn't twitched, I wouldn't have been sure she'd heard Pearl at all.

The tiny one continued unperturbed. "So that means a biped must have killed Tobias in the end. You didn't murder him after all."

I decided to come to Pearl's aid. She looked a bit overwhelmed by her unapproachable conspecific, who towered over her by more than a head.

"We—and our bipeds as well—suspect Ivo Lindquist," I told Bastet now. "We assume he completed your assassination attempt on Tobias, although we're not yet clear what his motive might have been. Was he trying to steal the Bastet statue? Or was it just a diversion? After all, he is rich enough to have bought a similar work of art for himself if he'd wanted to. And then he threw it away in the garden? It just doesn't add up."

I broke off because I realized that I had drifted off into a soliloquy to sort out my thoughts. But we had come to find out something from Bastet that we didn't yet know, not to indulge in further fruitless musings.

So I looked at her and yelped encouragingly. "You know something about this, don't you?" I probed.

Bastet wrapped her tail around her paws and once again gave me one of her poison-green looks, which felt like they could kill.

"Tobias has been taken out. That's all that matters," she said in a cryptic tone. She looked up at the branch of the beech tree, as if now planning to continue her interrupted nap up there.

"Ivo will surely be arrested by the police," Pearl said. "Is that what you want? Would you stand by and watch an innocent man go to jail, or did he actually kill Tobias?"

Pearl received no answer. Bastet began to preen herself, just as can be expected from a cat when she feels insecure.

I made one last attempt to get this arrogant creature to talk to us.

"You told us that you loved Tobias," I began. "Before you found out he was a monster—a monster who deserved to die, in your opinion?"

"I wouldn't have brought him down on the stairs otherwise, would I, smarty-dog?" the cat replied.

"But why, Bastet?" Pearl meowed, upset. "What did he do to you? Tell us already. We're not your enemies, damn it!"

Bastet's eyes widened at the gruff tone the tiny one had struck. Pearl reared up in front of the much larger cat, and puffed up her chest. Well, she had me as a backup, but I still found her behavior quite foolhardy.

Apparently, Bastet was also impressed. She made an annoyed sound, but finally deigned to share her knowledge with us.

"Ivo was Antonia's lover," she explained. "*That* was

his motive for killing Tobias, if he suffocated him as you claim. I can't testify to that, because after I brought Tobias down I disappeared from the stairwell. I didn't want to be seen, so that I would in no way be associated with his fall."

"So you didn't check if Tobias was really dead?" I asked.

"No. That wasn't really my point, either. I just wanted to ... incapacitate him."

"*Incapacitate him*? What are you trying to say, Bastet?" I cried. "Won't you finally tell us? What did he do, why was he such a monster in your eyes?"

I took a step toward her, quite unconsciously, but for her it probably came across as a little threatening. Nevertheless, she bravely held her ground. She merely narrowed her eyes and hissed warningly at me.

I stopped and lay down to signal to her that I had no attack in mind.

Pearl picked up on Bastet's assertion. "Ivo was Antonia's lover, you say. Did you see that with your own eyes?"

Bastet hesitated. She certainly didn't like her statement being questioned in this way. Once again, she looked up at the safety of her siesta branch.

But she stayed where she was, with us on the ground. She might be a murderer, or at any rate an assassin, but the idea of Ivo going to prison apparently did not appeal to her, even though he might actually have killed Tobias.

Was that due to her sense of justice? Possibly; most animals possess it. Pure malice and coldness of heart, as humans can sometimes display, is extremely rare among our kind.

But *why* did this cat consider the death of her human, whom she had once loved, to be just? I still didn't understand.

"We are not your enemies, Bastet," I repeated Pearl's words, giving her my most loyal puppy-dog look. I can't say why I did that—I certainly didn't want to cozy up to her, but kindness sometimes gets you further than you could hope.

Bastet eyed me from the side, but directed her answer to Pearl. That was fine with me; the main thing was that she finally talked to us.

"I didn't watch Ivo and Antonia having sex, if that's what you mean," she said, "but I heard them—at night in Antonia's room, when Ivo was a guest here at the villa, as he is now. She sleeps alone, after all, and Tobias did too. I'm not allowed to enter the bedrooms ... but I have excellent hearing."

"Wow," I snapped, "that's daring. Antonia cheated on her husband in his own home? And with one of his best friends?"

"They would lock the door when they met secretly in her bedroom," Bastet explained to me. "I heard that clearly every time. And in the worst case scenario, Ivo could certainly have climbed out the window if Tobias had shown up in the middle of the night and demanded entry to Antonia's room. From the first floor, and on a facade as heavily structured as ours, even a clumsy biped can climb down without seriously injuring himself."

Bastet's whiskers twitched, and she fell silent. She looked thoughtful and depressed. Why was she so preoccupied with the lives of her humans?

19

Pearl turned to me. "Do you remember what Leo told Victoria? That Antonia suffers from nightmares?"

Of course I hadn't forgotten. "Leo attributed it to the curse of the Bastet statue," I said.

"I guess he was wrong about that," said Pearl. "He was talking about hearing Antonia moaning and screaming through the walls, albeit quietly enough that only he overheard it, because he lives next door. I think he must have misinterpreted those sounds entirely."

"You don't mean to say that—" I began.

But Pearl cut me off with a question to Bastet: "When were Ivo and Antonia last together? In Antonia's bedroom, I mean."

Bastet did not have to think for long, and did not hesitate to give us this information. "That was one night before I made Tobias ... *you know*."

"Before you ran between Tobias's legs to make him fall down the stairs."

"Right." There was no trace of remorse; Bastet even seemed proud of her deed. Her motives were still clouded for me. Surely she had not wanted to murder her human so that Antonia could get together with Ivo?

"So that was the very night that Antonia supposedly

148

had nightmares again, according to Leo," Pearl said to me. "Now we know that she was in fact having sex with Ivo, and not for the first time. Also, I can see now why the friendship between Tobias and Ivo was so strained, or rather why Ivo was so strangely dismissive of his friend. He wanted Tobias's wife for himself, while Tobias probably didn't know about the affair and therefore continued to be friendly with his supposed closest friend. Or was he aware of the affair after all?" Pearl turned to Bastet and shot her an inquiring look.

"No, he didn't know anything about it," the cat said coolly. "He certainly wouldn't have stood by and watched it happen." Her expression darkened.

"Right," I said, "humans don't like it when their husband or wife cheats on them. They think they are monogamous, when in fact they are not."

"But still," Pearl objected, "I don't understand why Ivo killed Tobias. Antonia could have just divorced her husband, couldn't she? Why murder the poor guy?"

"The *poor guy*?" hissed Bastet—so unexpectedly that a startled squeak escaped Pearl.

"Tobias was not the one to be pitied, you clueless fool! Quite the opposite," Bastet snapped, angrily lashing out at the midget. "And Antonia would most certainly have divorced him if she'd have dared to. But then he would have killed her, you understand? He would have followed her to the ends of the earth, no matter where she fled from him. And then he would have snapped her neck, and I would have had to helplessly watch him do it. So if Ivo suffocated Tobias, completing my work at the foot of the stairs, it was only to help Antonia—to save her. He acted for the same reasons I did when I made Tobias take that fall."

Bastet's whiskers twitched angrily. Her green eyes glittered venomously at Pearl. I intervened, baring my teeth in warning before she could do any harm to my poor pipsqueak.

Bastet turned to me with a jerk and hissed again like a fury gone wild. "Do you think I'm afraid of you, you hulk of a dog?" she hissed.

Before I could react, Pearl jumped death-defyingly forward and gave the much larger cat a blow with her paw. Right on the nose.

That hurt, as I knew from my own painful experiences, and Bastet had not reckoned with such audacity—or should I say, such madness? She flinched reflexively.

High time to de-escalate the situation before we were all at each other's throats.

"Easy, girls," I grumbled placatingly, panting in a friendly manner and lying down in front of Bastet. A gesture of humility, but it was really necessary now. We were not yet at the end of our questioning, quite the opposite.

"We're all pulling in the same direction," I reminded

the green-eyed fury. "So you're claiming ... what, exactly? That Tobias threatened Antonia?"

I felt Bastet's hot breath on my snout. She was still standing upright, with her back arched high—but at least she relaxed a bit now.

Pearl stood next to me, also hunched up to her full height, but fortunately for all of us that didn't really look dangerous.

"He didn't just threaten her," Bastet said coldly. "He hit her, beat her up. Abused her. And more than once!"

"And you saw that?" I asked again.

"No. It also happened in Antonia's bedroom, behind closed doors. But I saw the injuries he inflicted on her—because she showed them to Ivo, secretly outside in the park, when they were alone. Twice she did that, at least in my presence. Once a few weeks ago when he was staying here at the house. The second time a few days ago. It all got worse, you see: at first Tobias gave his wife only a few scratches, a few bruises, but lately..." She lowered her head.

"I had to do something!" she said, looking up again. "I had to protect Antonia. She was suffering mortal fear!"

"So Tobias really was a monster," Pearl whispered, barely audibly.

Bastet hung her head. "I would never have believed him capable of it," she said just as quietly, suddenly sounding very emotional. "He was always so good to me, never harmed a hair on my head. But his wife—you would have protected her too, wouldn't you? You would have done the same thing I did, stopping him in any possible way."

Yes, probably, I thought to myself, but did not say it aloud. If someone had hurt Victoria, I would have morphed from a peace-loving dog into a killer wolf—even if that isn't really in my nature.

"So Ivo found Tobias at the foot of the stairs on the night in question," Pearl said, trying to process the new and quite unexpected information. We had to completely reassemble the picture we had gained of Tobias, his character and especially his death. "Ivo saw that Tobias was injured, maybe even unconscious, that he couldn't fight back..."

"And he took advantage of the opportunity," I continued. "To free his mistress from her abusive husband—and then he staged the burglary and the theft of the cat goddess to create a false trail. Presumably he knew that death by suffocation could be proven, and that merely faking an accidental death was out of the question. You see it on television all the time, how capable the forensic doctors of the two-leggeds really are nowadays. They find out almost everything. Of course, Ivo could not have known that the Bastet statue was of illegal origin—he simply threw it away, into the thistle thicket, and assumed that it would never be found again."

Pearl grumbled in agreement. "But when we did

track her down, thanks to the bat witness, that's when Julius wanted to make sure she disappeared for good. So no one could find out he'd acquired her illegally before selling her to Tobias."

Bastet suddenly took a step toward us. She still looked furious, but her anger was no longer directed against Pearl or me.

"You have to do something," she demanded firmly. "You must help Ivo—he may be a murderer according to the law of the bipeds, but he had a good reason for his deed! This policewoman must know about it, and you must not allow him to be locked up. That would be unjust."

In the next moment she made a giant leap, landed on the trunk of the beech tree and nimbly climbed up onto her siesta branch. She no longer hid her limp from us, but it hardly hindered her. Her injury seemed to be healing quickly.

She settled on the branch, enthroned like the goddess she thought she was, and looked down at us once more.

"Promise me Ivo won't go to jail," she demanded again. "You two are such super smart detectives, aren't you?"

"We'll do our best," Pearl said, but she didn't sound confident of victory.

How on earth were we going to achieve the impossible? How could we exonerate Ivo and explain to Melissa Funke why he had suffocated Tobias, making her see that there was a damn good reason that had driven him to the act?

Yet another insurmountable task.

Pearl and I returned to the house, ran into the kitchen, and I splashed around in the water bowl for a bit to calm myself down. Victoria often accused me of drenching half the room with water when I drank, which I thought was an outrageous exaggeration. But today maybe it was true, at least somewhat.

Pearl drank only a few sips, and then we both settled down on the kitchen floor to cool off a bit. I for one was in dire need of it.

"Oh, by the way," I finally said to Pearl, "thanks for defending me against Bastet's invective. Your paw slash was really impressive."

"You think so?" the tiny one said proudly.

"Absolutely!"

"Bastet deserved it. *Hulk of a dog*? How could she say that! Only *I* may tease you about your weight."

"My what?"

"Uh, I mean about your thick fur that makes you look a little ... voluminous," Pearl said hastily. But it didn't escape me how amused she looked at saying that.

I gave her a nudge—just a tiny bump—with my muzzle.

She rolled theatrically to the side. "Ow!"

"You're really too bold for your own good, Tiny."

20

A short time later the police returned, in particular Melissa Funke and Christian Wolf, as they had promised our two-leggeds on the phone.

The chief inspector and her silent assistant met Ivo just as he was coming down the big staircase in the entrance hall.

Pearl and I had also run into the hall as soon as we'd heard Melissa's car pull up outside. It was an older model that had a decidedly different engine sound compared to the luxury cars of the villa residents and guests.

"Excellent to have met you," Melissa said to Ivo as they crossed paths. "We'd like to talk to you in private, Mr. Lindquist."

"Talk to me? Again?" Ivo said, irritated. He wanted to hurry on, to ignore the policewoman's request, but Christian Wolf stepped in his way.

Ivo didn't like that at all. "What are you doing? What do you want from me?" His voice grew higher and shriller, and I could smell that he was seized by fear.

They want to arrest you because you are a murderer, went through my head. At least according to the laws of the bipeds. I had to think about Bastet, and that we had promised her to do everything we could so that

Ivo wouldn't go to jail.

Now, however, Pearl and I merely stood a little distance from the stairs, like two bronze statues that fitted seamlessly into Tobias Unruh's art collection, and didn't know what to do.

Victoria, Tim and Luisa came rushing from the corridor that led to the kitchen; apparently Melissa's arrival had not escaped them either.

Tim gave Ivo a wordless look, then walked up to Melissa and handed her a small envelope.

She opened it carefully, and I spied that inside was the dried-up burdock that Tim had picked from Ivo's pants.

The chief inspector nodded with satisfaction.

Ivo made a second attempt to go his way, but Melissa held him back. This time with words, and without her assistant having to intervene.

"Mr. Lindquist, would you like to accompany us to the station? There we could talk undisturbed if you don't feel comfortable here, and—"

"I'm not going to accompany you anywhere!" Ivo cut her off sharply. "What do you want from me? Am I under arrest? You have nothing on me. I'm going to call my lawyer—"

Melissa raised her hands placatingly. "You are of course free to do so at any time, Mr. Lindquist. But we're interested in having a brief conversation—I'd like to clarify a few points with you, that's all. You're not under arrest, at least not at this stage."

Pearl gave me a startled look. "What can we do?" she asked.

I did not know the answer.

"We'd also like to take a look at your guestroom here at the house, Mr. Lindquist," Melissa continued.

Ivo's odor of fearfulness increased. However he continued to act stubbornly, and tried to stand his ground against the policewoman.

"You'll need a warrant if you want to conduct a search, won't you?" he hurled at her. "Do you have one?"

Melissa's patience with the man seemed to be rapidly coming to an end. Her dark eyes fixed on him like those of a predator about to pounce on its prey at any moment. But she remained civil.

"We can always get the necessary warrant," she said coldly, but in a seemingly calm voice. "Believe me, it's not a problem at all. If you really want to complicate things...."

"What do you have against me?" Ivo tried to defend himself yet again. "What are you trying to pin on me?"

"As I said, we just have a few questions for you, Mr. Lindquist."

He opened his mouth, determined to protest further, but this time Melissa interrupted him: "If you'd like to discuss it here in front of everyone, that's fine by me. We were able to recover the stolen cat goddess, and found only two sets of fingerprints on it—

apart from a few isolated ones belonging to the owner. There were the prints of Julius Feldmann, which is to be expected after he stole the bronze statue from the garden when the dog was guarding it. However the second set matches yours, Mr. Lindquist, and you have some explaining to do in this regard. The statue was kept in a locked display case here at the mansion before it was stolen, and, according to witnesses, every time Tobias Unruh picked it up, it was carefully wiped down afterwards before being put back in its place."

She glanced briefly at Luisa at these words. Apparently the housekeeper was the witness in question.

"Moreover, we have been told that Mr. Unruh merely used to show the statue to his guests, but never put it in anyone's hands. Or would you like to contradict that, Mr. Lindquist?"

Ivo couldn't get a word out.

Melissa held up the envelope Tim had handed her earlier. "Also, here's another piece of evidence I'd like you to explain. Maybe you can clear the matter up— I'm certainly open to hearing your side of things."

Ivo did not ask what was in the envelope. He just stood there and stared at the policewoman, startled.

"As I said, Mr. Lindquist," she repeated insistently, "we'd like to ask you some questions and take a look around your room. But if you'd rather accompany us to the station, and insist on us having a search warrant..."

Ivo's resistance broke so suddenly that a startled whimper escaped me. He staggered down two steps as if he had been shot, then grabbed the banister and sank to the edge of the stairs like a wounded man.

"Tobias was a swine!" he cried out. "I had no other choice. Besides, he was as good as dead when I found him; I just wanted to make sure he never..." He broke off abruptly, dropping his face into his hands.

I could hear his heavy breathing, and his smell of fear had turned to despair.

"I had to save ... Antonia from him," he suddenly cried, jerking his head back up. "He was such a brutal bastard!"

Melissa looked confused, as did her assistant and the other bipeds who were in the hall with her. No one seemed to understand what Ivo was talking about.

But at that moment Antonia suddenly appeared at the foot of the stairs and walked toward Melissa. I had completely missed that she had entered the hall, so completely had Ivo captured my attention.

Behind Antonia I also spotted Seschat, pressing herself like a shadow against the wall next to the stairs.

Antonia strode a little closer to Melissa. "Mr. Lindquist is telling the truth, Chief Inspector," she explained in a brittle voice. "He was just trying to protect me." She rolled up the sleeves of her dress, revealing large mottled bruises and some reddened abrasions on both arms.

More than one of the bipeds present let out a startled gasp at the sight.

Melissa reflexively took a step back. She might have been a hardened police detective, but she clearly hadn't expected this turn of events. I saw compassion flash in her eyes. She would clearly have loved to rush up to Antonia and take her in her arms.

"My husband abused me," Antonia said. Her voice sounded like a dead woman's. "And his fall down the stairs was an accident. He was as good as dead when Mr. Lindquist found him. I'll take his word for that. Ivo just—he wanted—"

"I had to make sure he could never hurt Antonia again!" Ivo interposed.

Melissa swallowed. She exchanged a wordless glance with Christian, then found her powers of speech again.

"I'm still going to have to ask you to answer some questions for us, Mr. Lindquist. Albeit under different circumstances, now."

She did not give him a chance for renewed objections, but turned to Antonia. "Which room can we use?"

"The library, if you like," the woman replied. "Just take the passage on the left, you already know the way." She pointed to the appropriate corridor leading away from the hall.

"I will call my lawyer," Ivo said tonelessly. "You will have to be patient that long."

"No problem," Melissa agreed. "But in the meantime, take a seat in the library, would you?"

It was clear to me that she was not going to let him out of her sight. She didn't want to pronounce the arrest officially yet, although she had every reason to do so now. It was only a formality, because Ivo had confessed to the crime.

Antonia wanted to accompany Ivo, but Melissa wouldn't let her. "We will come back to you later, Mrs. Unruh—for your own testimony. Please be patient a little longer."

Antonia nodded mechanically, gave Ivo a last desperate look, then gathered the hem of her dress and ran up the stairs. Victoria and Tim followed her, surely to provide some kind of emotional support.

The two police officers disappeared with Ivo in the direction of the library. Only Seschat remained in the hall; she had merged so completely into the shadows that the other bipeds must have forgotten her presence. Now, however, she broke away from the wall, staggering like a drunk.

"Come on, she needs help!" cried Pearl—and was already setting off. She ran toward the girl, who had taken only a few unsteady steps and then braced herself again. There she sank to the floor as if paralyzed, and curled up in a heap of misery.

Pearl snuggled against her knees—which made Seschat wince.

"Oh it's you, little one," she sniffled.

She pulled Pearl to her and hugged her tightly. I approached her carefully, but saw that it was not necessary to make myself available as a cuddly toy as well. Pearl was fulfilling that function perfectly.

"I was ... so blind," Seschat said haltingly to the tiny one. "I had no idea that my father...." She shook her head. "That monster! How could he!"

Pearl let out a sympathetic mewl and Seschat squeezed her tighter.

Suddenly Victoria appeared behind us. Had she noticed Seschat after all, or remembered her presence in the hall when she'd already gone halfway up the stairs?

Tim was not with her, so he had probably accompanied Antonia, while Victoria wanted to take care of Seschat. She settled down on the floor next to the girl and put her arm around her trembling shoulders. A tiny, melancholy smile flitted across her lips when she saw that Pearl was already providing expert comfort.

"You—didn't know about what your father had done to your mother?" she asked Seschat gently.

The girl shook her head violently and sniffled. "Nothing at all. But I—I should have noticed! And I should've stood by Mum. If I had seen through my father, I would have pushed him down the stairs myself!" Anger flared up in her bright eyes.

"Now, now, dear, you really mustn't blame yourself," said Victoria.

"I should have known," Seschat insisted. "There—there were signs, looking back now. Just last week, I overheard a conversation. Just a few words, through my mother's bedroom door. Father asked her about some bruises. She gave him an explanation ... and it seemed believable to me! I'm such an idiot! Why didn't I see what it was all about?"

She suddenly pushed Pearl off her lap, jumped to her feet and ran up the stairs.

Victoria also got up, albeit much more slowly. She seemed to hesitate for a moment, to ponder whether to run after Seschat, but then decided against it.

She stood there very still, just for a few seconds. Then she patted my head, lost in thought, and finally climbed the stairs as well, but at a more deliberate pace.

I wanted to follow her, but at that moment I heard an excited chirping. It came from one of the windows, which was standing wide open and letting warm air into the house.

There on the ledge between the two window wings sat a small, rather ruffled sparrow.

21

The sparrow chirped excitedly and fluttered its wings. "Has the two-legged been arrested now? Is he a murderer? I can't believe I've gotten to see something like this in real life!"

I approached him, Pearl following behind me, and the little fellow was so tired of living that he actually stayed perched on his windowsill.

"Hello, little one," I said good-naturedly, "you should be careful not to become a murder victim yourself ... with all the enthusiasm you obviously have for crime."

I didn't intend to threaten him, but merely to issue a warning. The little fellow was a few weeks old at most, hatched this summer, and he seemed never to have heard that cats have a very special fondness for small birds like him—an extremely unhealthy one, from a bird's point of view.

He looked at me excitedly, not a bit intimidated.

"I've never seen a dog as big as you," he chirped. "Did *you* make sure that biped was arrested?"

"Well, my cat and I did." I lowered my head to Pearl, and the sparrow followed my gaze.

"She's so small," he said. He really was tired of living. "Beautiful white color, though! Gorgeous coat," he added quickly as Pearl narrowed her eyes. "I've been watching you two for several days now. You've been investigating, haven't you? Like two professional sleuths."

"Yes," Pearl said in a charitable tone, "we helped expose this biped as a murderer ... but in this case, I don't think we can celebrate it as a success."

"Why not?" the curious fledgling inquired further. "Oh, wow, I can't believe it—you guys really are two actual detectives. I'm such a lucky bird, it's such an honor to meet you guys!"

He whistled, chirped, jumped up and down, and I honestly wondered why he hadn't already fallen off the windowsill dead with all the excitement. Straight into Pearl's mouth—not that she would have deigned to eat a sparrow. She was too much of a gourmet for that.

"I grew up with all the two-leggeds' thrillers, you know," the chatty bird continued, unasked. "My nest was over there, on the other side of the valley, in the garden of a few old ladies. They used to sit together under a tree, knitting and listening to those so-called audio dramas. Crime stories, that is! I listened too, of course. It was sooo fascinating."

He stretched his wings, looked at his ruffled feathers for a moment, then retracted them. "Oh well, my childhood was really exciting."

I refrained from pointing out to him that he had barely outgrown his childhood. At this point I wanted to end the conversation with the cheeky bird in order to consult with Pearl. We needed a plan in case Ivo really was arrested, and by now that seemed inevitable. Would the humans in the courtroom acquit him because he had merely been defending Antonia with his deed? Or would they still consider him a murderer who had to spend many years behind bars? A whole dog's life long....

Terrible idea; it made the hair on the back of my neck stand up.

Neither Pearl nor I knew much about human jurisprudence. Of course, we'd watched one or two judicial thrillers on television, but that was it. Would we be forced to come up with some insane plan to get Ivo out of prison?

I could think of absolutely nothing in that regard; it was clearly out of our league....

The sparrow, meanwhile, continued to chirp on unperturbed. "Those old ladies in our garden, they were very kind. They used to feed my parents and the other birds of our clan, and scold their cat-beast when it killed one of us. It was a real monster, that cat—"

He fell abruptly silent and squinted down at Pearl. "Oh dear, I didn't mean to offend you. I'm sure you're a really nice cat who doesn't eat sparrows, right? But the old ladies, they had this huge cat, with tabby feathers..."

"Fur," I corrected him. "It's called fur. Only birds have feathers."

"Oh, right. I did know that," the youngster chirped

happily. I had to hide my amusement from Pearl, who by now was staring at the guileless little chatterbox as if she really did want to eat him.

"Why are these bipeds so violent toward each other?" the sparrow asked abruptly. "Surely you, as detectives, must have figured it out. And sometimes even against themselves! That's crazy, isn't it? Like that woman, for example, who lives here in the house."

He paused for a moment, and the sudden silence did my ears good. But it was only short-lived.

"She is very strange, that woman," the sparrow philosophized further. "Humans are supposed to be monogamous just like us, aren't they? But she kisses other men."

Again I swallowed a remark, which was on the tip of my tongue, namely that female sparrows in particular are well-known for not taking monogamy all that seriously. After all, I didn't want to disillusion the little bird, who might soon start looking for a partner himself.

"Ivo hasn't been arrested yet," Pearl grumbled. "And we'll know how to prevent that."

She raised her head, looking at me piercingly. "He wouldn't be the first biped we've helped to escape, would he?" she said.

I wanted to say something back to her, but suddenly I heard the last words of the sparrow once again in my head—as if they were echoing in my skull.

"What did you just say?" I snapped at him.

His eyes widened. Had I growled at him in my excitement and finally scared him? It quite looked like it.

"I'm sorry, kid. You mentioned something about the woman who lives here..."

"Her name is Antonia," said the sparrow, a little more timidly than before.

"Yes. I know that."

"She is unfaithful to her husband. Yet humans are monogamous, they claim. She—" He was chirping away blithely now, as he had done before. The big, dangerous dog—yours truly—had apparently only intimidated him for a very short time.

"That's not what I meant," I slowed him down. "You were yakking, er, talking, about people hurting each other. And themselves, too. You implied Antonia was hurting herself...."

"Oh, I see. Yes, yes, I heard that. Here in the park, from some friends...."

"Other sparrows?"

He looked at me uncomprehendingly. "Of course other sparrows."

What had I expected? Squirrels?

"And what did they see, your friends?" Pearl interjected. She'd probably understood right away that this statement was very strange.

"Well, that Antonia hit herself here in the garden, with a stick. Funny, isn't it? It happened near the laurel hedge, by the little pond. That's where my friends live. Want me to show you the way?" He fluttered up excitedly.

22

Sparrows are the ultimate gossips. *The sparrows whistle it from the rooftops*—this saying has not found its way into the bipeds' lexicon for no reason.

Pearl and I did not hesitate for long. I put my front paws on the windowsill, pushed myself up and jumped outside. Pearl made a huge leap—by her standards—and also made it to the window ledge. She landed almost silently next to me on the grass.

"Onward, young sparrow," I urged our new friend, "show us the way!"

We trotted away from the house, chasing after the little guy, who was flittering through the air in front of us like a drunken bumblebee. His flying skills could definitely be improved upon.

"Maybe Antonia was trying to learn self-defense," Pearl said to me as she galloped beside me. "To be able to protect herself from her brutal husband. Maybe that's what those sparrows were watching—her training."

"And beat herself up in the process?" chirped the sparrow that was fluttering above our heads. The little guy never seemed to be at a loss for words.

Pearl said nothing in reply.

A few moments later we'd already reached the laurel hedge our young friend had spoken of. A whole colony of sparrows seemed to live here. Some of them rose, startled, into the air when Pearl and I approached them.

But the youngster confidently landed on a twig and announced, "Don't worry, guys. My two friends are detectives. They investigate among the bipeds. Isn't that wildly exciting?"

Chaos broke out. Dozens of sparrows suddenly started chattering like crazy, flapping their wings excitedly, buzzing around my skull....

I did not understand a single word.

In the next moment, the foolhardy youngster rose from his branch, flew over to me—and actually landed on my head. *The audacity!*

"You really are a good-natured house dog," I heard Pearl murmur. "A wolf would have eaten that little fowl by now."

"Too many feathers," I replied.

"Will you ask your friends about Antonia, please," I addressed the fledgling.

He tried, and they listened to him for a moment, but then chaos broke out again. Even louder than before. I picked up only a few words.

"Cane ... blows ... right over here ... must have hurt like crazy ... witnessed it several times."

"When was that?" I asked the group aloud.

More deafening chirping followed.

"Maybe I can help,"—I suddenly heard a dark voice at my paws.

I lowered my head, unintentionally catapulting the youngster toward the hedge. Fortunately he remembered his wings in time to avoid a crash landing. He headed for a nearby branch, looking a little flustered, and then puffed himself up like Pearl when something didn't suit her. *Too funny.*

The voice at my feet belonged to a fat toad.

No, wait, no one should be offended here because of their weight! So a well-fed, stately toad.

"I can give you a report," she said, "before you lose your minds with this sparrow chorus—or indeed your hearing."

She hopped confidently towards me. She didn't seem to be shy of Pearl, either. Her species is not on the menu for dogs or house cats, and she apparently knew that only too well. The skin of many toads supposedly secretes a poisonous substance that not only tastes disgusting, but might even be dangerous to a tiny creature like Pearl. I know this only from hearsay, though; I have never attempted to lick a toad myself. I like to leave such experiments to my more foolhardy contemporaries, because our constant murder cases are thrill enough for me.

"This woman the sparrows talk about ... she's been here," said the toad, "more than once. She hid behind the hedge I suppose because she didn't want to be seen by the other two-leggeds from the house."

A flapping of wings interrupted the toad's report. The youngster landed directly between us in the grass. Really, he was a suicide candidate. His curiosity would soon cost him his life if he continued like this.

"Never land on the ground," I warned him. "You're the most easy prey if you are down there."

But he turned a deaf ear to my well-meaning words.

"Told you!" he chirped excitedly. "Didn't I? That Antonia comes here to hurt herself. I'm a good detective too, don't you think?"

"You have potential," I said good-naturedly. "But you really should pay more attention to your safety. The only good sleuth is a live one, you know."

"What? Oh, I see. Yeah, you're right." He looked around, apparently finally remembering the lesson from his parents, who had surely drilled into him the same thing I had just tried to do. Namely, that sparrows on the ground are absolutely defenseless victims.

With an awkward flap of his wings, he took to the air and actually had the audacity to land between my ears again. I sighed inwardly, but at least the fellow now held his beak, and the toad could continue her report.

"It is true that the woman hit herself," said our amphibian witness, "and to answer your question, dog, as to when that happened ... the last time was only a few days ago. Shortly afterwards, I think it was the very next day, she showed her injuries to this man who is rarely here in the garden. I don't think he lives in the villa."

"Ivo Lindquist? Very lean and quite tall...."

"Yes, that's him. She did call him Ivo, I think. And a couple of times *darling,* too, as far as I remember."

The toad chortled. "For me, the lives of the bipeds are not as insanely interesting as they are for sparrows, you know."

"Sure," I said quickly. "As a toad, you have, uh, more important things to do."

I sensed her sympathetic approval.

"But we're still glad you watched the two bipeds," Pearl took over the conversation. She was pretending to be a polite kitten, not the prickly beast she could be at times.

The toad looked at her with an expression of admiration in her round dark eyes. Apparently Pearl could even steal the hearts of amphibians, and not just those of bipeds.

"Antonia and Ivo," I picked up the thread again, "what were they doing here?"

"They were cuddling. And the woman showed him her wounds—the ones she had inflicted on herself. Scratches, bruises ... the skin of the bipeds is really pitiful. It can't stand anything. However, the woman complained about her husband, how brutal he was. That his attacks on her were becoming more and more heinous. *I can only hope for a miracle,* she said in tears. *Tobias is not advanced in age yet, and he is in good health. He won't just die; he would have to suffer an accident ... only then can I be free. He would never agree to a divorce. Oh, Ivo, we'll never be together, and I do love you so!"*

The toad fell silent, while the sparrow on my head began to flutter wildly. He hopped up and down excitedly, his tiny claws tickling me.

"Sit still!" I commanded.

He obeyed. "A real whodunit, isn't it?" he chirped, utterly overexcited. "Like one of those radio dramas my old ladies were so fond of. Only it's for real! So gross!"

"Quiet," I growled. "How is one supposed to concentrate with all this noise?"

"Sorry." The sparrow didn't move around anymore and actually shut its beak.

"Am I mistaken, or did this woman incite her lover to murder her husband?" the toad asked me.

23

"Quick, Athos, we have to get back to the house!" I heard Pearl's sharp voice next to me.

We thanked the foolhardy young bird and the toad, and ran off. The whole flock of sparrows that resided in the laurel hedge rose excitedly into the air once again, and followed us a little further in the direction of the house.

When we spotted Tim and Victoria, who seemed to be stretching their legs a bit on the front lawn of the villa, we ran up to them and the sparrows took up strategic positions on bushes and trees. They probably didn't want to miss what was happening now, and would surely chatter about it for weeks to come.

Further back, on the terrace in front of the dining room, we spied Antonia sitting alone on a chair with her shoulders slumped, holding a large steaming cup in her hands.

Fortunately she hadn't noticed how excited we were as we ran towards our humans. We didn't want her to end up getting the idea that everything here revolved around her.

Apparently the conversation between Melissa Funke and Ivo Lindquist was still going on in the library, or at least I hoped so. We had to make it clear to Melissa—and to Ivo—that he had been set up. That Antonia had put him up to the murder of her husband, and not because he had been abusing her.

It was all so confusing.

Fortunately for us, we'd noticed that Tim and Victoria were also discussing the case. She was holding onto his arm, but was gesticulating excitedly with her free hand. She smiled briefly when Pearl and I appeared, but it didn't interrupt the flow of conversation, which was just fine with me. Neither Pearl nor I were looking for cuddles or kind words—we were here to unmask a murderess!

"Seschat's statement just doesn't make sense to me," Victoria was telling Tim. "I mean, Tobias was asking Antonia about her bruises ... why on earth would he do that when he'd supposedly inflicted the injuries on her himself?"

Tim merely nodded. It seemed as if the conversation had been revolving around this question for some time, and he had long since run out of answers.

Victoria stopped and bent down to Pearl, because she was grumbling loudly at her. She took the little one in her arms, then looked at Tim questioningly.

He hunched his shoulders. "It's not like I can make sense of it either, sweetie; I've told you that already. But what could be behind it? Did Seschat lie to us and make up this conversation between her parents?"

"For what reason?" asked Victoria. "No, I think she was telling the truth."

She cuddled Pearl's head gently, lost in thought,

while I feverishly racked my brain as to how we should inform her of the true state of affairs.

Pearl beat me to it with a theatrical performance that was absolutely stage-worthy. One moment she was sitting upright on Victoria's arm, the next she was collapsing like a dead doll.

"Pearl!" cried Victoria, startled. "What's the matter?"

Pearl got up again, touched Victoria's nose with hers, then repeated her act. Again she fell lifelessly on Victoria's arm, with which she was carrying her, and stretched out all fours.

"She's playing dead," Tim muttered.

"Yes, but...." Victoria stammered.

I yelped excitedly to emphasize that Pearl and I had something important to tell our humans.

Victoria looked at me questioningly. "Do you want to show us something, you two? Come on, where do we have to go? Run, Athos!"

I sat down demonstratively on my hind paws. Running was not the order of the day right now. There was no place where we could lead our two-leggeds to reveal the truth to them. We had to *talk to* them.

Tim and Victoria were now both staring down at me. "What's going on, Athos? Is it about—the murder of Tobias?" asked Victoria.

Tim laughed out, looking half amused, half terrified. "You do realize how crazy that question is, don't you?" he said to Victoria.

She contorted her face in embarrassment. "Yes, of

course. Athos is a dog, and Pearl's a cat. But you know how they've been in the past ... in those other murder cases. Oh, I don't know. Sure it's crazy; we can't humanize them like that." She fell silent.

Pearl uttered a plaintive meow, then dropped dead again.

"She's playing dead," Tim muttered, "but what's she trying to tell us? Surely Tobias didn't fake his own death ... but who else could she mean?"

"What were we talking about when Athos and Pearl showed up?" said Victoria, more to herself than to Tim.

Nevertheless, he answered her, "About Seschat—that she may not have told us the truth."

"Is that what Pearl is implying with her playing dead? That the girl was lying?" Victoria began to chew on her lower lip.

Pearl sat stiff as a bronze statue, staring at Victoria. I could sense her frustration, which was an echo of my own. Trying to talk to the bipeds really was futile.

"Hmm, Pearl shows no further reaction," Tim said, eyeing the tiny one and me intently.

He abruptly slapped his hand against his forehead. "Just look at me, Victoria. Now I also expect them to understand us. That they can answer us...."

I opened my muzzle and licked Tim's hand. "Yes, human, I can understand you. Just wrap your head around that thought, please. It's urgent!"

A warning came to my mind that my mother had

given me and my siblings when we were still small helpless puppies. The same warning that is probably instilled in every animal with their mother's milk ... or with their first earthworm, or whatever they may eat: *you must never let the two-leggeds know how intelligent you are. That you can understand them, while they think you are a stupid, instinct-driven creature. Humans can't stand this truth, so you mustn't reveal it at any cost. It could be very dangerous....*

But now the time had come to throw Mother's well-meant words to the four winds. If Pearl and I longed to be detectives, and if we wanted to solve this intricate murder case, we had to communicate with our two-legged helpers. Otherwise a murderer would get away without punishment: Antonia.

I looked into Tim's eyes. I read in them astonishment, confusion—but also the irrepressible desire to understand me. No matter what he might have learned from *his* mother about communicating with animals.

"So it's not about Seschat?" asked Victoria.

Pearl and I remained motionless.

"About Ivo, maybe?" ventured Tim. His gaze bore into mine.

We continued to stare at the two of them in silence.

"Think about it," Victoria exclaimed, seized by sudden excitement, "if Seschat is telling the truth, if she actually heard her father ask Antonia about the bruises ... that must mean he didn't know how those injuries occurred, right?"

Tim nodded hesitantly.

"And that, in turn, must mean that it wasn't Tobias who inflicted them upon Antonia."

"But who else could have?" asked Tim.

Pearl repeated her feigned death act once more. Then she nudged Victoria excitedly with her tiny nose. I emphasized the urgency of her message with excited barking.

Victoria looked just as startled and confused as her boyfriend did, given the fact that Pearl and I so obviously wanted to talk to them, and about a very specific topic too.

"Playing dead," Tim said slowly. "Faking death..."

"Not death," I yelped excitedly, "just her injuries! Antonia wasn't wounded by Tobias." But of course the two-leggeds couldn't understand me.

In the next moment, Pearl did something that, in my eyes, finally elevated her to the highest echelons of the art of acting. She got back up after her latest playing-dead maneuver and fixed Victoria with her baby-blue kitten eyes. But there was nothing young, innocent or even naive in them now. Just wild passion and determination.

That I would ever have said something like that about the midget....

But that's how it was. And that was not all; Pearl lifted one paw, flashed her tiny claws—and then ran them over her own face, very slowly and deliberately.

My breath caught in my throat.

And Victoria finally understood. "She's scratching herself ... oh my God, Tim, she's pretending to hurt herself. That must be it!"

It took him a little longer than his girlfriend. "What on earth are you talking about?"

"Antonia. Her injuries are self-inflicted!"

Pearl excitedly slapped her tiny tongue in Victoria's face. I joined her in drooling all over Victoria's hand. "Way to go, human! You got it!"

Victoria, startled, withdrew her hand from me, while at the same time she stretched the arm Pearl was sitting on a little away from her body, as if this limb suddenly didn't belong to her anymore. As though Pearl were an alien who had just materialized out of nowhere, in her grasp.

On the one hand, our poor human looked extremely excited, because the truth about the murder case had finally revealed itself to her, but at the same time nameless terror was written all over her face.

"Tim ... how can this be?" she stammered. "Am I losing my mind? Athos and Pearl—they can't really understand what we're saying, can they? Or even tell us anything all that complex. But they just...."

She set Pearl down on the ground and pressed herself against Tim's shoulder. He put his arm around her, but again sought my gaze.

I whimpered softly.

"I'm sorry," I said. "We really didn't mean to scare

you, but it was necessary. You understand that, right? You have to hunt Antonia down; Ivo killed Tobias, but he acted in good faith. He wanted to protect her, just like Bastet did. But Antonia put him up to it, she made him her murder weapon, and she can't get away with that!"

Tim shook off his trepidation. He grabbed Victoria by the shoulders.

"I don't know what just happened here, either," he said, "but I think we've realized something crucial: Antonia was just faking that Tobias was hurting her. That makes sense! I would never have thought him capable of such brutality; he was such a quiet, peace-loving man."

"Which doesn't have to mean anything," Victoria muttered. "But I also think Antonia was just playing us—or Ivo, rather." She cleared her throat and made an obvious attempt to pull herself together.

"Even if it's really true, Tim, how in the world are we going to prove this to Ms. Funke? We have nothing to show her except these clues from our pets."

She ruffled her hair and shook her head. "But we can't stand by either, and let only Ivo be punished. I'm sure he was acting in good faith when he killed Tobias. He wanted to save Antonia, with whom he is obviously very much in love. Did you see the way he looked at her earlier? That was the look of a man who would do anything for a woman. And she must have taken shameless advantage of that. She talked him into believing that her husband was abusing her—and to what end?"

"So he'd take him out," Tim said. "Why else put on that awful show? What normal person would fake something like that?"

Victoria nodded. "That's right. So Antonia is our real murderer. She manipulated Ivo, that poor, unsuspecting guy, into playing the noble knight for her. She can't get away with that, Tim!"

Tim's eyes widened. "I have an idea," he said slowly. "Maybe it's somewhat crazy, but...."

"*Somewhat* crazy?" Victoria repeated. "And you think that might scare me off right now?"

She squinted down at us, to where we were sitting on the floor, well-behaved and quiet as befitted two tame—and utterly stupid—pets. Just the way the humans wanted us to be. We couldn't subject Victoria to another shock, otherwise she really would lose her mind. And that really mustn't happen to a psychotherapist, of all people.

My mother's warning had not been in vain. Nevertheless, I had no regrets—*we* had no regrets, I should say, because Pearl looked as determined as a wild lioness. Now it was up to Tim and Victoria to expose Antonia, and I was counting on them not to disappoint us.

Tim immediately set about explaining his idea to Victoria: his somewhat crazy plan, as he had called it.

"Well, I'm going over to Antonia to keep her a little

184

busy so that she doesn't get the idea of going into the house and checking on Ivo. After all, his questioning has been going on for quite a long time now. You, on the other hand, must do the following, please...."

24

As agreed upon, Tim walked to the terrace outside the dining room to join Antonia.

"You go with him," I said to Pearl, "so we know what's happening there. I'll accompany Victoria."

For once Pearl did not protest. She trotted after Tim when he left us, and I joined our other human, who made her way into the house.

Victoria was looking down at me as if she was seeing me with completely new eyes. As if I were a stranger, an alien. I didn't like that at all, but it couldn't be helped now.

She hurried into the entrance hall and from there straight toward the library, where Melissa and her assistant were questioning Ivo Lindquist. She knocked briefly, but at the same moment let herself into the room.

I stayed close on her heels. She began to put on a show that wasn't bad either—almost as good as Pearl's had been earlier in the garden.

I saw that a young man in a suit was sitting next to Ivo. He had on a serious expression, and was looking at me in fright as I trotted into the room behind Victoria. Probably the lawyer who had arrived in the meantime.

"Dr. Adler?" Melissa looked surprised. "We're still

not done here, I must ask you to—"

She didn't get any further, because it was time for Victoria to put on her act. She suddenly had tears in her eyes and when she started talking—or rather sobbing—I hardly recognized her voice. It sounded tearful, shrill and completely hysterical.

"Antonia, that bitch" she howled, "she ran off with my Tim! She bewitched him, stole his heart, took him away from me!"

She hurried toward Ivo and plopped into the vacant chair next to him.

"She fooled us both, Ivo," she cried as she grabbed the stunned man by the shoulders and shed more tears. "You and me. That Tobias beat her, abused her—it was all lies! She just wanted to be rid of him without giving up his fortune, and she took advantage of you to do it. I suppose there was a marriage contract between her and Tobias, and if she had divorced him, she would have come away empty-handed." The assumption was obvious, although to my knowledge Victoria had no proof of it.

Ivo backed away from her as if she were a madwoman. "What are you talking about?" he asked breathlessly.

Ms. Funke jumped up. I saw conflicting emotions flash across her face: on the one hand, she certainly wanted to get Victoria out of the room as quickly as possible, because she really had no business being here. But on the other, what Victoria had claimed was clearly interesting for the policewoman.

Victoria took advantage of the resulting delay and continued, sniffling: "I overheard everything! Antonia confessed to Tim what she's done. What her diabolical plan looked like, which she so successfully put into action. You were just her stooge, Ivo. The fool who did the dirty work for her so she'd be free for someone else. And she chose Tim, of all people, as her new lover. She's had her eye on him ever since we arrived here. I just didn't want to believe it—I'm such a stupid cow. And now she's taken him away from me. He ran away with her, was completely blinded by her, even though she is a murderer. That snake!"

She pulled a handkerchief out of her pants pocket with shaky fingers and blew her nose loudly.

"That's a lie!" roared Ivo. "Antonia loves me. She—"

The lawyer resolutely put his hand on Ivo's arm. "You'd better keep quiet now, Mr. Lindquist."

But Ivo was not to be tamed.

"Antonia would never lie to me," he exclaimed.

He pushed Victoria away from him as if she disgusted him and raised his voice even further. "Tobias, who I thought was my friend, was abusing Antonia!" he cried. "God knows for how long it had been going on, even though she only recently confided in me in her agony. Because she was desperate, the poor woman! I saw with my own eyes the injuries Tobias had inflicted on her."

"She hurt *herself*, Ivo," Victoria insisted. She was no

longer crying, having probably run out of tears, but she was still eminently believable in the role of the jilted woman whose boyfriend had fallen for the dark charms of a madwoman.

"Get this woman out of here," Ivo's lawyer demanded of Melissa, but she still stood motionless, listening spellbound to Victoria's accusations and Ivo's impassioned rejoinders.

I figured I should underline the drama of the situation with some yapping—and so I did just that.

The lawyer looked at me, startled, and for a moment forgot about trying to get Victoria to leave, so I could chalk that up as a success, but unfortunately nothing more.

Victoria made another attempt to portray Antonia as a faithless traitor who had abandoned Ivo and run off with the next best man.

But he did not believe her, no matter how much she implored him. "Antonia would never lie to me. Or even worse, betray me," he announced in a booming voice.

Then he turned to Melissa. "I killed Tobias. All by myself; Antonia had nothing to do with it. I will swear to that in any court in the world. The poor woman is innocent, a helpless victim, I tell you!"

The lawyer made a last desperate attempt to prove himself useful. "Mr. Lindquist, you really shouldn't..."

But Ivo silenced him with an imperious gesture. "I don't need your services anymore! Not here, not now.

You can take over my defense in court, but I will not allow poor Antonia to be turned from victim to perpetrator—over my dead body!"

Turning to Melissa again, he added, "The idea to kill Tobias was *mine*. I didn't plan the deed, but when I found him that night at the bottom of the stairs, already half dead, I had to seize the opportunity..."

"So you didn't push him down yourself?" asked Melissa. "You're sticking with that statement?"

The lawyer leaned back in his chair and pressed his lips together. *Go ahead, talk your head off, you idiot!* his angry glittering eyes seemed to say. He made no further attempt to help his client.

"I stand by the statement," Ivo said solemnly. "It's the truth; Tobias was badly injured, perhaps he would have died anyway even if I hadn't intervened. *Cursed Bastet*, he muttered when I found him, but he seemed very dazed to me."

"He was talking about the cat statue?" asked Melissa. "So then he actually believed in a curse, as does his father...."

I knew better. *Cursed Bastet* referred to the house cat that had run between his legs at the top of the stairs, causing him to fall. A willing murderer who had been deceived by Antonia, just as poor, faithful Ivo had been.

Apparently Bastet had never followed her mistress into the garden on those occasions when Antonia had hurt herself, and therefore had not seen through her hoax.

Presumably, if I had questioned the sparrows—or rather the toad—further, I would have found out that Antonia used to wound herself precisely at times when Ivo was visiting the house. And once, her husband had probably seen the bruises—which of course had astonished him. Seschat had overheard that conversation....

We had all fallen for Antonia, even Bastet, who believed herself to be a goddess.

"I was just doing my civic duty, nothing more," Ivo announced, having by now really talked himself into a groove. "I stand by what I did—yes, damn it, I should have pushed Tobias down those stairs myself! You can't just look the other way when a man commits such violent acts as he did to his poor wife. You have to act, don't you? And that's exactly what I did. And yes, I love Antonia ... now I don't have to hide that from the world any longer. Besides, I know that her heart belongs to me, forever. No way she's run off with that—that wannabe historian, that gardener!"

The lawyer groaned softly, but said nothing more.

"You, Mr. Lindquist—or Mrs. Unruh herself—should have called us in," Melissa said. "You don't just take justice into your own hands as a law-abiding citizen. An assault charge would have been the way to go. Instead of committing murder."

Ivo laughed bitterly. "Oh yeah? In the hope of what, exactly? Tobias would have been given a few measly years in prison, if that. And afterwards? Antonia would no longer have been safe, no matter where she went, where she tried to hide! Apart from the fact that a wealthy man like he was could have pulled the necessary strings even from inside prison. He would have taken his revenge on Antonia, and I couldn't let that happen under any circumstances."

Melissa ended the drama. She now formally arrested Ivo, and he offered no resistance. Christian Wolf took it upon himself to bring the man—and his defense attorney, who had at least stayed with his stubborn protégé—to the station.

The chief inspector took Victoria to task. "So Mrs. Unruh admitted to you that she had hurt herself? You heard that with your own ears, or did your boyfriend just tell you that? And did he really run off with her?"

Victoria's face crumpled like a puppy dog's that had just peed on a priceless carpet. An expression that I'd rarely observed on her before.

"Well, you know...." she stammered.

Melissa looked at her sternly.

"They didn't really elope," my human admitted. "And they're not having an affair, either. Tim is in the garden with Antonia. On the terrace—or maybe they've been stretching their feet a bit."

"Excuse me?"

"I—we—I just wanted to draw Mr. Lindquist out with my performance. We—that is, my boyfriend and I—are convinced that Antonia set Ivo up, and I wanted to get him to see that."

"What was he supposed to admit? That he was set up? That doesn't make any sense."

"That Antonia instigated the murder of her husband. So that she can at least be punished as an accomplice—for incitement to murder or whatever it's called."

Victoria hung her head. "Now Ivo will take the punishment all by himself and Antonia will remain at large, where she can fully enjoy her husband's fortune, which she will now inherit. It's just not fair...."

"Wait a minute," Melissa interrupted her. "Now what evidence do you have to support your accusations? Mrs. Unruh has not admitted any of the things you're claiming here to you, has she?"

"She hasn't," Victoria muttered meekly.

"Then what makes you even think that she hurt herself and thus incited Mr. Lindquist to murder?"

Victoria hesitated. She gave me a meaningful look, which I returned faithfully.

To Melissa she said, "Because of Seschat. The girl told us that Tobias asked Antonia about her injuries. That he was quite amazed at her bruises. That proves he had no idea about them, doesn't it? That he couldn't have inflicted them on her! Why don't you talk to Seschat yourself?"

"That's what I'm going to do," Melissa said. "And what else?"

"What ... else?" asked Victoria, confused.

"What other proof or circumstantial evidence do you have for your accusations, apart from this vague remark by the girl? I hope I don't have to explain to you of all people that Seschat must be under a severe state of shock due to the events of the last few days?"

Victoria swallowed. I could see the predicament she was in: what else was she going to tell Melissa? That her pets had gone crazy trying to let her know that they suspected Antonia?

I could do nothing but sit by Victoria's side and give her moral support with my presence.

Should I have yelped at Melissa, put my paw on her knee to vouch for Victoria's words? That was futile. And the testimony of sparrows or toads was equally worthless in a human court.

"You should have talked to me in private," Melissa said in an accusatory tone to Victoria. "Instead of barging in here and putting on this show!"

"I wanted—I hoped that I could draw Ivo out with that. That he would incriminate Antonia when he had to assume that she had left him for another guy."

"What a crazy idea! You only came up with that because you knew full well that you don't really have anything on Mrs. Unruh ... except for those few words of Mr. Unruh's that Seschat claims to have overheard."

Victoria nodded hesitantly. But then her fighting spirit awoke, it seemed to me. She had not given up yet.

"Can't you interrogate Antonia, using your methods—until she caves in and confesses?" she asked the policewoman.

"Using *my methods*?" repeated Melissa, drawing out each word. "What do you have in mind? Do you want me to put thumbscrews on her, or waterboard her for a bit? If this woman is truly guilty, as you claim, then she is a master manipulator and has committed the perfect murder. I do hope you realize that. You have seen Mr. Lindquist's dog-like devotion to her—do you really think that such a woman will confess voluntarily? With everything going like clockwork for her?"

I had a strong objection to her use of the word *doglike,* but saw zero opportunity to voice my complaint.

Victoria was silent as well. She certainly saw that Melissa was right in her assessment of Antonia's personality.

"You'll talk to Seschat, won't you, Chief Inspector?" she finally repeated in a rather pitiful tone. She seemed to know that she had already lost.

25

When it came, it fell like a doom knell. When Victoria called Melissa again later that afternoon to inquire about the conversation with Seschat, the policewoman reacted coldly and curtly.

Victoria, as usual, put her phone on speaker so Tim could listen in. Of course Pearl and I also pricked up our ears, even though we tried hard to lie there seemingly bored and dozing off. We didn't want to further unsettle our two-leggeds by letting them know that we could follow a phone call.

"Of course Seschat didn't incriminate her mother, but I'm sure you didn't expect her to," said Melissa. "The girl may not be particularly close to her parents, as is the case with most teenagers, but when you've just lost your father you don't send your mother to prison."

Victoria's voice sounded hoarse as she answered: "So that means Seschat denied that she overheard her parents' conversation? Where her father wondered about Antonia's injuries?"

There was a pause: Melissa was probably debating with herself whether she should give any more information to this annoying psychologist, who in her eyes must be quite unhinged. As far as she was concerned, the case was probably closed. She had a perpetrator who had confessed—what more could she want?

Whatever might have caused Melissa to stay on the line and not just arbitrarily hang up after all, she finally said, "Seschat stated that she wasn't sure exactly what she'd heard. The door was closed, she couldn't really understand everything, et cetera. Nothing usable. And you should go home now, Dr. Adler, you and your boyfriend. There is nothing more for you to do here. Also, I really hope that this is the last criminal case you get involved in."

She sounded as if she felt some sympathy for Victoria and her efforts to help with the case. She said goodbye in an almost friendly tone, then hung up.

Tim and Victoria stared at each other. Then Victoria's gaze fell on me and Pearl. Not even the tiny one felt like contradicting the policewoman's statement and hoping for numerous future criminal cases that we would be allowed to solve in our lifetimes. The defeat we had just taken really hurt.

"What do you think?" Victoria asked Tim. "Should we really head home? Have we gotten carried away by something that might only exist in our imagination?"

"That Antonia put Ivo up to the murder, you mean?" said Tim.

Victoria nodded hesitantly.

"No," Tim protested, "that's not a product of our imagination. I think we're absolutely right in our suspicions—but it doesn't matter now, because we can't prove anything against Antonia."

"We have been influenced by the strange behavior of our pets," Victoria said. She avoided looking at Pearl or me with these words. "It can't really be that they are capable of such intellectual feats, and that they understand our language so well. I think we've gotten ourselves into something here, Tim, because we have been so eager to be detectives."

"As I said, it doesn't matter now anyway. We can just leave the matter to the police, and they will see to it that Ivo is charged. He will probably get a lenient sentence, because he acted from motives that are well understandable. He thought Tobias Unruh was a monster."

"But in truth, Tobias was nothing of the sort," Victoria protested. "He did nothing wrong—but was killed in cold blood by his own wife. Surely we owe it to his memory that he at least be cleared of this hideous slander, if his murderess does get away with it."

"Well. And how are you going to do that?"

Victoria didn't know the answer to that. Tim pulled her into his arms and gently stroked a strand of hair from her forehead.

"I guess it doesn't always work out when you try to be a private investigator," he said. "There are failures, too."

Victoria grumbled something unintelligible, but had obviously conceded defeat.

"Let's leave tomorrow, shall we?" said Tim.

"Alright." She looked down at me with a furrowed brow and lots of unspoken questions in her gaze.

I did my best to look like a guileless and somewhat sleepy dog, even though I would much rather have made it clear to her that Pearl and I were also struggling over our shared defeat.

"It was a mistake for us to reveal ourselves to Tim and Victoria like that," I said to Pearl when we were back amongst ourselves. "Humans just can't handle it. It turns their whole worldview upside down."

"I guess that's right," Pearl said. She was in a bad mood, not being used to taking failure in her stride.

"We have one more thing to do before we leave. We need to tell Bastet the truth," I explained, trying to get her mind off our defeat. "She has a right to know that her master wasn't really a monster after all."

"But her mistress is one, all the more," said Pearl. "She won't like that either."

"No, definitely not. But still, I want her to know what really happened."

"She made the wrong person fall down the stairs." Pearl's eyes narrowed. "Are you going to tell her?"

"Oh, so the inconvenient missions get to be undertaken by the dog, huh?"

"She might tear my head off," Pearl said meekly. "And you don't want that, do you? Seeing as you're my bodyguard."

"Let's go find her," I said.

Bastet had made herself scarce, probably roaming around in the park or in the adjacent forest. She'd apparently had enough of the two-leggeds for the time being—for which one could not blame her.

We found her not far from that laurel hedge where we had met the flock of sparrows. She was lying on the marble pedestal of a pharaonic statue and seemed to be sleeping. But when we approached her, first her ears twitched and then her whiskers followed suit. She perceived our presence and finally opened her eyes.

Pearl sat down solemnly in perfect silence and let me do the talking. *The little coward!*

I didn't know how to proceed other than to get straight to the point.

"Bastet, your human was not a monster," I said to her, and went on to explain everything in detail. That Antonia was not a poor, defenseless victim of domestic violence, but that the injuries she'd blamed on Tobias had in fact been self-inflicted. And that she had beguiled Ivo Lindquist into killing her husband for her. "And she fooled you, too, Bastet," I added.

After a moment's hesitation, I went on, "You have nothing to blame yourself for; you acted in good faith and wanted nothing more than to protect her."

Bastet did not comment on my report with a single word. When I had finished, she closed her eyes again ... just as if she now wanted to continue her interrupted nap.

However, I saw—and smelled—that she was in great turmoil inside. Outwardly, only her ears were moving, twitching back and forth, but she did not let me share in her thoughts, in the pain she surely had to be feeling.

"Let's go," Pearl murmured to me. "I think she wants to be alone right now. There's nothing more we can do for her."

We left in brooding silence.

Even though I hadn't really warmed up to Bastet, I felt sorry for her. She had fallen for Antonia's lies and intrigues, as we all had. Tobias, whom she had once loved, had become the victim of the most heinous slander, and Bastet had at least participated in his murder. Would she ever be able to forgive herself for that?

Shortly before we reached the villa, we met Victoria, who had just settled down at the large dining table on the terrace.

Dusk had long since fallen, but apparently there was no dinner planned in the garden today. The two-leggeds, including the cook, seemed to have finally lost their appetite.

Only Leo was sitting at the table, all alone, looking old and exhausted. He was wearing workout clothes and sweating profusely, so I assumed that he had once again worked hard on himself under the eye of the trainer, Giorgio.

Pearl and I ran to the two bipeds. She jumped on the old man's lap and let herself be cuddled.

"I'm going to miss this little girl," Leo said as he gently stroked her fur. "She's really adorable."

"She is," Victoria said. "And so is Athos in his own way."

Nice of her not to forget about me, but that wasn't really important at the moment. My mood was at its lowest point.

Our first murder case in which we've completely failed, I said to myself, probably for the tenth time in the last few hours. The sense of defeat just felt terrible.

26

Victoria and Leo were not exactly in high spirits, either. However, she was apparently not yet ready to truly admit defeat and allow Antonia to triumph.

"Who will inherit the house now?" she asked the old man casually. "And the beautiful Egyptian collection?"

"*Beautiful*?" Leo frowned. "Well, if you say so. I never could get into that stuff. All the magical hoopla, the mummies, the hideous gods with their animal heads...."

"Will it all belong to Antonia now?" Victoria inquired.

Leo nodded, lost in thought—I couldn't tell if he had actually registered the question. He wiped the sweat from his forehead with the back of his hand. His breathing was heavy and irregular.

It occurred to me that perhaps the man was going too far with his training, that he was overexerting himself, because he smelled more sick than healthy to me.

Luisa suddenly came outside through the patio doors, which by now looked like new again. She was carrying a tray, and served Leo a large salad bowl and a glass of water.

He thanked her, but did not start to eat.

Pearl jumped off his lap and joined me. The sight of so much green stuff was probably unbearable for her.

"You really do follow a very strict diet," Victoria remarked. "Your discipline is admirable."

He started poking wordlessly at his salad.

"Regarding the house," Victoria said. She twisted her lips into an embarrassed smile. She was clearly not comfortable asking such persistent questions, but she was still not ready to give up.

Leo lowered his fork.

"The house," he said, lost in thought, "goes to Antonia, of course. The collection, too, and then the other assets will be divided between her and Seschat. Antonia must hold everything in trust until the girl comes of age."

Victoria took a deep breath. She smelled extremely tense, and the next question she asked Leo was visibly even more uncomfortable than the previous one.

"If there had ever been a divorce between Tobias and Antonia," she began, "did a—um—a prenup exist for that eventuality?"

"Why do you want to know?" Leo asked suspiciously.

"Forgive me—I'm just terribly curious." She couldn't think of anything better to say.

Leo shrugged. "I myself advised Tobias on the prenup, back when they were getting married. I got the impression...."

Suddenly there were tears in the corners of his eyes.

He leaned back in his chair.

"Oh, hell! At the time I thought Antonia was a calculating floozy, a gold-digger as they say, who was only after my son's fortune. And now...."

He sniffled, indignantly wiping the tears from his cheeks. "Now I have to realize that my son was a scumbag who mistreated the poor woman. God knows how long he'd been torturing her. And I never noticed, even though I lived under the same roof. I will never forgive myself for that."

Victoria leaned forward and put her hand on his. "You're really not to blame, Leo," she assured him. Then she fell abruptly silent.

"A man who beats his wife," Leo exclaimed. "Is there anything more cowardly, more shameful?"

He had apparently heard nothing of the accusations that Victoria had made against Antonia this morning, as Luisa had not been in the house at the time we had burst into Ivo's interrogation. She had gone shopping, so no one had overheard the conversation and subsequently passed on the information within the house.

I could see that Victoria was struggling with herself, that she was feverishly thinking about how she could still bring the whole truth about Antonia to light.

But finally she seemed to come to the conclusion that the old man could not help her with that either, and that therefore it would only be inhumane to torture him further with the death of his son.

"So is your daughter-in-law going to stay here in the

house, or sell the property?" Victoria asked cautiously.

Leo reached for his fork again, but didn't continue eating. "I think she will stay here, at least for now. For my part, however, I shall move out as soon as possible, although Antonia would certainly continue to accommodate me. She's really quite lovely; I did her a terrible injustice with my initial suspicions regarding her intentions. But now that Tobias is gone, there is nothing to keep me in this Egyptian—"

He struggled to find the right words. "In this tomb, this *mausoleum*. The house is now not only filled with mummies, but for me it's also full of the memory of the collector of those abominations ... who now himself walks in the realm of the dead. Fortunately I don't believe in that nonsense, but the Egyptian ritual, where some goddess tests the hearts of men for their guiltiness by weighing them against a feather—Tobias would not pass it. Which means ... oh, I have no idea. Was there such a thing as hell among the ancient Egyptians?"

"I'm afraid I don't know," Victoria said.

"Well, never mind. He's dead anyway, gone long before his time. Before I myself bit the dust ... I never dreamed that would happen."

"At the end of the day, it can happen to any of us," Victoria said. "At any time, no matter how unexpected. Death is the only certainty in our lives, isn't it? But it's also totally unpredictable."

"That may be so," Leo suddenly exclaimed. "But I won't give in so easily! I'll fight for every hour, every day I have left."

He pressed his lips together resolutely. His muscles were rigid with tension.

A tired old warrior who would not give up, went through my head. Who would fight until his last breath.

I really was in a melancholy mood that such thoughts were coming to me. But there was nothing I could do about it.

"Carpe diem," Leo muttered to himself. "And you're only as old as you feel."

"Wise words," Victoria said, but then she suddenly looked Leo straight in the eye. "Excuse me for asking you this so directly, but—are your days truly numbered? Are you suffering from a disease that..."

"What makes you think that?" Leo interrupted her. "Have you been spying on me? Or is Luisa an even bigger snoop than I thought?"

"No, not at all. I just noticed from the beginning how hard you fight for your health, for every day of your life. Generally, only people who know that their time on earth is limited do that. The rest of us live rather carefree, day to day, often wasting the time we have available...."

She smiled apologetically. "I'm a psychologist, you know. Or rather, I was," she corrected herself after a brief pause. She left it unsaid that she had spied on

Leo while he'd been visiting a suicide forum.

Had he done research there in order to be able to take his end, when it finally came, firmly into his own hands? Such a wish would have suited him, the fighter that he was in my eyes.

"Which is it now?" asked Leo. "You *were* a psychologist, or you *are* one?" He seemed eager to turn the tables and pepper Victoria with questions instead of answering hers.

Victoria smiled wanly. "I don't know that yet myself. But from my experience so far, I know people who have reacted either with apathy or with an irrepressible will to live when they realize that their time on earth is limited."

Leo nodded as if in slow motion. "I chose the will to live. And you're a good observer."

He turned his head toward her, eyed her carefully. "I have colon cancer. How mundane! My son wanted me to undergo chemotherapy, but I rely on alternative methods. Among other things, on exercising my body and on eating nothing but healing foods."

"I understand," Victoria replied in a sympathetic tone.

"So *that's* what the argument between Leo and Tobias was all about," Pearl said to me. "His son threatened to kick him out if he didn't finally see reason and follow the doctors' recommendations. Tobias wanted his father to undergo this *chemo-thingy* therapy. That really doesn't sound very appealing to me."

"Two-legged doctors are not necessarily omniscient," I heard myself say.

What a strange remark. Since when was I an expert when it came to human medicine?

The only striking thing is that our dear bipeds supposedly have the best medical care among all the inhabitants of the earth, but suffer from more diseases than any animal I know.

Leo began to slowly eat his salad. But between bites, he continued his conversation with Victoria.

"You must be good at your therapist job," he said. "Sensitive and understanding—at least, that's how you strike me."

"Thank you, I'm glad to hear that."

"Whatever you may decide as far as your future career is concerned, just make sure that you and your nice young man enjoy every day of your lives."

He looked down at Pearl and me and added: "Your animals are also a blessing that will only be granted to you for a short time. I have always found it most unjust of our Creator—if there really is one—that he has measured the lives of our pets in so short a span. Our Bastet is also getting on in years, but cats at least have around twenty, twenty-five years on earth. Your dog, on the other hand...."

He shook his head. "He still looks young, but if you're very lucky, he'll only have fifteen years. Then his death will tear an incredible hole into your life."

"I really don't want to think about that right now,"

my human said softly.

Leo nodded his understanding, then silently finished his salad while Victoria stared off into nowhere.

Pearl and I stretched our paws a little. Leo's words about my very short lifetime had made me melancholy.

The pipsqueak did not miss that. Pearl could also be sensitive, if she wanted to be.

"Cheer up, Fatt— uh, Athos!" she tried to raise my spirits. "If you die before me, you'll just have to come back as a ghost and stay by my side. No problem at all, right?"

"Do dogs become ghosts, too?" I thought aloud to myself. It wasn't the first time I'd asked myself that.

"Of course, why not?" Pearl replied in a tone of conviction.

"I've never met a dog ghost before," I pointed out. "And you probably haven't either."

"We'd never seen a human ghost before ... until the moment we ran right into one. And that wasn't so long ago."

I knew what she was alluding to: in our last murder case, we'd actually had to deal with a haunting.

"In any event, I'm counting on you, Athos. Promise me you won't abandon me just because you're going to die one day. According to you, I need a dog bodyguard, don't I?"

"I'm rather doubtful whether I'd make a good protector as a ghost."

"What are you talking about? Of course you would! You could scare the hell out of any scoundrel who'd want to hurt me."

"You really think so?"

"You probably wouldn't make for such a comfortable pillow, though," Pearl mused. She trudged along beside me like a little philosopher, having to take three steps every time I took one just to keep up with me, but she didn't let that faze her.

Oh, Tiny, I'll definitely come back to you as a ghost. I couldn't imagine being without this prepotent little pipsqueak, who thought she was a royal tigress and an expert on just about everything.

"As ghost detectives, though, we'll have an even harder time taking down criminals," Pearl babbled on as we took one of the gravel paths that led deeper into the park.

Then at least no villain could hit me over the head with a bronze statue, I thought to myself. That would clearly be an advantage.

"So that means you would also return to me as a ghost?" I asked Pearl. "In case you should die before me?"

Pearl stopped and narrowed her blue eyes to slits. "Sure thing—point of honor. In any case, I'm definitely not going to take my rightful place as a cat in the heaven of the gods right away, but I'd rather be haunting the humans with you for a good while. I'm sure it'll be fun."

My melancholy was no match for so much self-confidence and unshakable good humor. I lowered my head and front paws and invited the tiny one to play. "Come on, midget, a round of tag! You'll never catch me!"

27

When Pearl and I at last came back to the house, Victoria and Leo had long since left the terrace. The evening was already far advanced; even in the villa's great hall, only the animal-headed statues of the gods were standing around and looking down on us menacingly. No biped was to be seen or heard.

We ran to the kitchen to drink some water, and maybe scrounge a snack should Luisa still be around in spite of the late hour.

The door was merely ajar, not closed. Pearl and I squeezed through.

There was no sign of Luisa, but Giorgio the fitness trainer was standing in front of the large refrigerator, pouring himself a glass of orange juice. Bastet was crouched on top of the huge appliance. She stared down at us as we entered the kitchen, but didn't dignify us with a word.

I didn't mind. Everything there was to say between us had already been said.

Giorgio walked over to the table and dropped down on one of the chairs, as if he were quite tired. He drank his juice in big gulps and suddenly tapped the seat of the chair next to him with a grin. As he did so, he looked at Pearl and said, "Come on, cutie, want to join me?"

Pearl did not.

Giorgio shrugged his shoulders. But before he could feel sorry about the rejection the tiny one had given him, the kitchen door opened a little further and Antonia slid into the room.

She smiled. "Ah, you're still here—perfect. I was afraid I'd missed you."

She pulled the door shut behind her and approached Giorgio. "How did it go with Leo today? Tedious as usual?"

"What?" asked Giorgio. His look seemed unfocused. "Oh no, not so bad."

Antonia's smile widened. "The others have all gone to bed," she said, emphasizing each word as if she were proclaiming news of national interest.

She paid no attention to Pearl, me, or to Bastet. Her gaze was fixed on Giorgio, wandering first over his face, then over his shoulders.

She quickly covered the short distance to the table and took a seat on the chair that Giorgio had originally intended for Pearl.

The next moment she did something completely unexpected: she wrapped her arms around Giorgio's neck, pulled him to her and kissed him passionately.

Behind me I heard a soft—but all the more threatening—hiss. It had not come from Pearl, as I'd first suspected, but from Bastet, who was still squatting on top of the refrigerator.

Antonia either hadn't heard it or wasn't interested

in her cat's opinion. She only had eyes for the fitness trainer.

"My love," she chirped, "at last everything is settled. Nothing can keep us apart now!" She kissed him again.

And what did he do? He returned her caress, even if perhaps he didn't look quite as infatuated as she did.

When they'd released each other from their embrace again, Giorgio said, "So this Ivo fellow, he must have had a huge crush on you. I still can't believe he committed murder for you, that he killed Tobias just like that, and will now spend years in jail for it."

"Insane, isn't it? I wouldn't have expected that in a hundred years!" replied Antonia.

"You didn't—you know, have something going with him or anything, did you, sweetie?" Giorgio asked jokingly.

She chuckled like a teenage girl and nudged him on the arm. "What, are you crazy? You think I'd cheat on you with some fuddy-duddy academic? Really, honey!"

What a hypocrite.

Giorgio looked in the direction of the door. Was he afraid that some inhabitant of the house might show up after all?

I pricked up my ears and listened, but could hear no footsteps approaching, and no other suspicious noises either.

Giorgio seemed to come to the same conclusion. At

this late hour, there was no danger of his love affair with Antonia being exposed. Apparently the two of them had successfully hidden this relationship from all the inhabitants of the villa, although it did not seem as if it had started only recently. Even Bastet, who was staring down at them with narrowed eyes, seemed to have been kept in the dark successfully.

If looks could kill. The house cat glared down at the two like a vengeful goddess.

"Why didn't you ever tell me that your husband was abusing you?" asked Giorgio as he stroked Antonia's hand. "After all, I've asked you a few times about your injuries, and you've always claimed you got them while playing sports. Which always seemed strange to me—you know that."

"Yes, darling, but you would have gone up against Tobias for sure, my sweet hothead. And then everything would have only gotten worse."

"I would have confronted him, that's true," Giorgio replied. "Given him a taste of how it feels to be beaten up by someone stronger. But I certainly wouldn't have murdered him!"

"I know, sweetheart. *I know.*"

She kissed him again. "Now we're free at last. No more clandestine meetings on the run, or in some shady hotel room—now we can finally be together. Forever."

"She set us all up!" Pearl hissed in my ear. "Not just her husband, whom she had murdered, but Ivo too.

216

She was just using him. In truth she wanted to hook up with Giorgio all along—without having to give up her husband's fortune. What a bitch!"

"It seems to me that Giorgio is rather more interested in the fortune than in Antonia herself," I replied. "In any case, he wouldn't have committed murder to save her."

"And she *did know* that," said Pearl. "That's why she took advantage of Ivo. She seduced him, making him believe he was her great love, until he was willing to go to extremes for her."

"And he was totally sure of her love, right to the end," I said. "Otherwise Victoria's little ruse would have worked after all, her lie that Antonia had run off with Tim, and Ivo would at least have admitted that Antonia had put him up to the murder."

Somehow I had to admire this historian, this fuddy-duddy academic, as Antonia had so disparagingly called him. He was so loyal, and his love so unconditional, that he'd sacrificed himself for another human being. Almost like a dog.

"What are we going to do now?" groaned Pearl. "Antonia can't get away with all this! Not with having cheated on poor Ivo, too—and letting him go to jail for her while she builds a new life with Giorgio."

"I think Giorgio is just going to take advantage of her, if that's any consolation to you," I said. "I mean, he's even fooling around with Antonia's daughter at the same time! It can't be true love. He just wants her money and maybe a little fun."

Before Pearl could answer, Bastet suddenly landed on the floor next to us with a huge leap. For a moment she stood there like the bronze statue of the goddess that Tobias had loved so much, but then she lifted her tail steeply into the air and strutted past us.

28

That night Pearl and I hardly slept a wink. We had suffered a total failure; for the fourth time in our lives we had managed to unmask a murderer, but this time the despicable biped would get away unpunished.

It may have been Ivo's hands that had ultimately suffocated Tobias, and Bastet had also played her part in his demise, but the real mastermind was without a doubt Antonia. And she could now look forward to a bright future in which, with a young lover at her side, she would squander her husband's money.

Victoria and Tim were just as depressed as we were, although they did not even know the full extent of Antonia's guile. Our two-leggeds had no idea, and would probably never know, that she had only used Ivo as her murderous henchman, but in truth desired the trainer, Giorgio. Pearl and I had agreed that we should not make any further attempts to communicate too clearly with our humans.

So the two of them packed their bags early in the morning and then decided to head home right after breakfast. Here at Villa Unruh, there was nothing they—or we—could do further.

Tim and Victoria walked silently hand in hand down the stairs to the ground floor, to share a last meal with the household. Pearl and I remained at the top of the landing, though, because Bastet had just emerged from one of the corridors. She was silent and regal as ever. She did not run down the stairs, but stopped abruptly and pricked up her ears.

From the corridor from which she had come, I could hear human footsteps rapidly approaching us.

Antonia appeared: she had her long black hair pinned up in a perfect knot, wore a shimmering blue dress, an overlay in the same color, and pearl jewelry on her neck and ears. She had also put on a heavy perfume that smelled intensely of roses and jasmine and which almost took my breath away.

Pearl let out a low hiss, but the lady of the house was in a good mood and paid no attention to us at all. She passed Bastet, then the two of us, and prepared to walk down the stairs in her high-heeled shoes.

A deadly she-devil.

Undoubtedly she was also going to the breakfast room. As she placed her left foot on the top step and lifted her right to descend the next one, Bastet suddenly raced at her from behind. She was fast as a cheetah and did not make the slightest noise on her soft paws. At least none that a human being could have perceived.

Bastet ran straight between Antonia's legs—sealing the fate of the vile murderess who had thought herself so victorious and invincible.

Antonia wildly flailed her arms, stumbled and reached out for the banister in a panic ... but it was too late. She could not catch herself, but fell head-long down the stairs.

The wood of the steps groaned and popped several times while Antonia tumbled down, bouncing so hard that I could hear her bones crack. In the end, she was left motionless and completely silent at the bottom of the stairs.

Bastet took up position at the top of the staircase and looked down at her. She narrowed her eyes, arched her neck—then suddenly turned and walked away with a measured stride.

Pearl and I rushed down the steps.

Downstairs, the first bipeds had already appeared, clearly alarmed by the heavy thumping on the stairs.

At night while everyone was asleep, such a noise might have gone unheard in most of the house, but a group of people in broad daylight in the nearby dining room had been inevitably alerted.

Victoria knelt down next to Antonia's motionless body and felt her pulse.

"She's alive!" she exclaimed after a few moments. "She's just lost consciousness. Call an ambulance, quick!"

"We mustn't move her!" said Tim, who'd appeared next, side by side with Leo. Close behind him followed Seschat, who burst into tears with shock.

"We are indeed cursed," Leo complained. "These stairs are really not dangerously steep or anything. And yet...."

There was nothing for us to do down here, so we quickly ran back up the stairs. Bastet had long since disappeared; none of the humans had seen her, but we managed to track her down.

She was sitting in a small room that looked very Egyptian, but which was not filled with the usual displays and showcases full of treasures. There were only a few of the typical columns, and the walls were decorated with paintings and hieroglyphics.

Otherwise the room was empty. I couldn't help but think of the temple that Tobias Unruh had apparently built here.

"My human liked this room," Bastet said softly as we approached her. "We used to come here often, whenever he needed some rest or to think about an important decision. He liked to lean against one of these pillars, look at the hieroglyphs, and then he'd usually talk to me as if I were a human being. A good friend who always had an open ear and gave comfort...."

"You avenged his death, Bastet," Pearl said. "That was very brave of you. But Antonia survived, and she'll probably remember that *you* brought her down. She may deport you to the animal shelter, or worse...."

"You don't think I want to stay in this house a moment longer, do you?" Bastet said in disgust. "With this two-legged *beast*. What could keep me here now?"

"You want to run away?" I asked.

"Of course. Let's see where Leo will move to—I'll roam around for a bit, and then maybe I'll join him again at his new home. I think he could use a little company now that he's lost his son. And maybe he'll take at least part of the collection to his new house. I have to say that I kind of like these Egyptian treasures. Especially the mummies."

The fur on the back of my neck bristled.

Bastet turned to the tiny one. "I could also follow in your footsteps, little Pearl, and become Leo's catfluencer. I think I would enjoy that. It's good to be duly admired as a cat by many, many bipeds."

For the first time I perceived something in Bastet that could be called a touch of humor.

While I was still thinking this thought, she became serious again. A somber expression settled on her beautiful, gray-speckled face.

"If Antonia survives, I will not rest until my work is complete," she said solemnly. "She will not get away with her heinous murder, and her betrayal of me. She made me believe that my human was a monster, and I went so far as to want to kill him for her sake."

"Are you not afraid that people will eventually figure out that you're acting with full intent in your attacks?" asked Pearl. "And that they will then ... euthanize you?"

Pearl had horror written all over her face. The word *euthanize,* even the mere thought of it, triggers about the same feelings in us animals as the different variations of human death penalties do in the bipeds when they talk about the subject.

Pearl earned a disparaging look from the much larger cat. "We are gods, little one, you should never forget that! The humans can't really touch us. We are above their laws, yet wise and just. And without fear."

Pearl said nothing in reply.

A few days after we'd left Villa Unruh, Pearl and I finally learned how Antonia had fared after Bastet's attempt on her life.

Victoria had stayed in contact with Seschat, as well as with Leo, to give them both emotional support, and in return was informed about any news from the hospital. And of course we pets listened to each and every phone call.

Antonia had survived the fall down the stairs, but she had been in a coma ever since. The doctors predicted that the chance of her ever regaining consciousness was very small, and even if she did, she would be in need of professional care for the rest of her life due to her severe injuries.

Paraplegic, was the word Victoria repeated to Tim several times, always shaking her head with a serious expression.

"It's kind of strange, that fall down the stairs, don't you think, honey?" she said afterward. "I'm really not a fan of *an eye for an eye, a tooth for a tooth,* but don't you think—well, that Antonia got what she deserved?"

"Absolutely," Tim said, "although I still don't understand how anyone could fall down those stairs. And Antonia certainly wasn't pushed, was she? All the house's residents were in the breakfast room with us, after all."

Victoria nodded. "No, I guess it was just a tragic accident. Albeit fitting in a most eerie way."

In the days and weeks that followed, we learned that Leo was staying at his son's house after all, together with Seschat, because he wanted to take care of the girl until she came of age.

So Bastet was able to keep not only her roof over her head, but also the Egyptian collection she was so fond of.

In addition, a few weeks later, Leo reported that his latest checkup at the hospital had given him reason for hope. In fact, it looked like he was well on his way to beating cancer.

I was very happy for him, and I could also picture the proud, regal Bastet perfectly in the role of catfluencer, which she would now certainly take at Leo's side. Secretly Pearl missed the job, I was sure of it, but she never complained about it once.

Giorgio remained Leo's fitness trainer, but we heard nothing to the effect that he'd become closer friends with Seschat or even her official boyfriend.

Good thing, I thought. He was hardly the right man

for the young girl. After all, he had cheated on her with her own mother!

We did not hear a word about Giorgio visiting Antonia in the hospital either, not even once. Of course no one noticed, because the humans didn't know about his secret relationship with the cold-blooded murderess. Apparently he was not the type to remain faithful to his lover in difficult times. I hadn't truly expected it, and I thought that it really served Antonia right, even if she wouldn't have noticed visits to her sickbed anyway.

Thus in the end this terrible murder case came to its conclusion, even though Pearl and I had failed in many ways. The murderer might have escaped human jurisdiction, but she'd received a punishment that was harsher than any prison term.

Ivo Lindquist, on the other hand, got away with only three years in prison, because everyone thought that he had merely protected an abuse victim and killed a violent criminal. I wished very much for him that after serving his time he would find a woman more worthy of his unconditional love than Antonia Unruh.

Tobias's reputation remained ruined forever in the eyes of most people, but I preferred to imagine him somewhere in the Egyptian underworld, where he didn't give a damn about the world of the living, and could be close to his beloved animal-headed gods.

It was a shame though that his body had not been

mummified—he would certainly have loved such an honor.

More from Alex Wagner

If you enjoy snooping around with Athos and Pearl, why not try my other mystery series, too?

Penny Küfer Investigates—cozy crime novels full of old world charm.
Penny only has two legs, but she's a feisty and clever young detective. 😊

Murder in Antiquity—a historical mystery series from the Roman Empire.
Join shady Germanic merchant Thanar and his clever slave Layla in their backwater frontier town, and on their travels to see the greatest sights of the ancient world. Meet legionaries, gladiators, barbarians, druids and Christians—and the most ruthless killers in the Empire!

About the author

Alex Wagner lives with her husband and 'partner in crime' near Vienna, Austria. From her writing chair she has a view of an old ruined castle, which helps her to dream up the most devious murder plots.

Alex writes murder mysteries set in the most beautiful locations in Europe, and in popular holiday spots. If you love to read Agatha Christie and other authors from the Golden Age of mystery fiction, you will enjoy her stories.

www.alexwagner.at
www.facebook.com/AlexWagnerMysteryWriter
www.instagram.com/alexwagner_author

Cover design: Estella Vukovic
Editor: Tarryn Thomas

Printed in Great Britain
by Amazon

34370785R00131